BEAT THE CLOCK

"Poisoned?" Dee asked. "Dr. John, what do you mean?"

"I mean *bacillus botulinus,* and that's a cute little poison, believe me."

"Oh!" It was the housemaid Lorraine, who cried out sharply. "Miss Lalia! I saw her eating the stuff this morning! And now she's gone. She's run away. Poor sweet little thing. Will she die?"

"The symptoms of this damn stuff don't show up at all for sixteen hours," Dr. John said. "If in that time we shoot the antitoxin to her, it'll be okay. You've got until midnight to find her. But if you don't . . ."

"We'll find her," said Dee grimly.

CATCH-AS-CATCH-CAN

CHARLOTTE ARMSTRONG

ZEBRA BOOKS
KENSINGTON PUBLISHING CORP.

Chapter One

The blue convertible wound upward. To the right and left the city infiltrated the valleys; it crept up the mountains. Behind, it spread and flattened toward the sea, miles to south and west, where the ocean curled and slapped the shore, where the sand would be crisp and hot, and the breeze salt-clean.

"We picked a day to get away," said the dark-haired man.

"A fine day," murmured the red-haired girl. The breeze stroked her bright hair. The September sun was a mantle on her shoulders. She was pretty sure they would not get away.

"We should take Laila with us," she said suddenly.

"We'll take your cousin Laila, if you insist." His voice was cooler than it had been.

"It's mean to run away from her, especially when we're going to the beach."

"Maybe. But if little cousin Laila is going, you and I can't talk, Dee."

"Talk?"

"Since the minute your Uncle Jonas showed up, three months ago, there have been complications. I think we're going to have to talk."

Dee Allison's hair had the colour and shine of a new penny but her skin was clear and fair with no rust of freckles. Her eyes were cobalt. Andy Talbot said her colouring was a blinding thing. He claimed that her photograph in black and white would reveal a perfectly beautiful stranger. Nothing now altered the spectacular quality of her looks. But she felt chilly in the sun.

"It's high time," Andy said. "You know that as well as I do."

The car missed a familiar turn. "Where are you going?"

"Up the hill."

"Andy, it's nearly one o'clock."

"You can give me twenty minutes. I've got things to say."

"All right," she said.

The car bent into the hills, entering the park. Dee watched the wild brush. For once she did not want to study lovingly the lines of Andrew Talbot's face, the inverted triangles of his brows, the thoughtful creases around the fine grey eyes, or the long inquisitive line of the nose. She had fallen in love with him as if she'd been struck by lightning. She had only just come out of school and into the business world when she ran right into the lightning bolt, the electric crackle that crossed the desks and the paper work between her and this dark-haired engineer, this Andrew Talbot.

It all went by threes, Dee was thinking. Three weeks after she saw him, his ring snugged down upon her finger. Three days later, Jonas Breen came home. With complications. Three months ago.

Jonas was dead, now. Her heart still mourned him, her fabulous uncle, the rover, the trader, who came and went unpredictably in an old-fashioned freedom. Dee had adored him for the splotches of colour he had cast into the orderly days of her childhood. She had not seen Jonas for four years. He never wrote a letter but descended on the heels of a cable or telegram.

Now, Dee remembered the windy evening at the airport and herself waiting between Andy's tall silence and the tall volubility of her cousin, Clive Breen. She remembered her own mood, her mind at ease after the scramble of opening Jonas's house, of hiring a chauffeur, a maid, to help old Mrs. Vaughn who had spent the long solitary years there as caretaker. She remembered joining with Clive to tell another tale of Jonas, happy that Andy was going to meet him, looking forward, looking forward to the sight of him, herself.

She had been happy then. Not since. Not quite. Uncle Jonas had not come alone.

The plane put its wheels on the markers. Then Jonas came, a big man in a dark overcoat, with a free-floating stride that denied his sixty-odd years. Dee had seen nothing but his face and the grey tufts of his eyebrows lifted just as she so fondly remembered them . . . until, embracing her, he said in her ear, "Dee, there's a surprise. Here's my little girl. Your cousin, Laila."

Dee lifted astonished eyes to see standing at Jonas's left a large well-fleshed, middle-aged woman in black clothes, hatless, with a pale countenance that was somehow over-size. This creature said, at once, in a sonorous voice, "Ah, not I. I am Pearl Dean. Are you well, Miss Allison?"

Too shocked even to whisper, Dee had turned to see Andy smiling down on a small person at Jonas's right, a girl she'd never seen or heard of in her life before. She was about eighteen years old, tiny and slim, with brown shy eyes under delicate level brows in a face of pure ivory, with an incredible cascade of hair that fell all the way down her back to her neat narrow little waist and hung, soft and dark, looking as if it had never known a pin or a lotion but was as easily perfect as a bird's wing.

Clive found a voice. "Why, say, Uncle Jonas, you don't mean to tell us!" he croaked. "This is your daughter?"

"I do," said Jonas. "I do. She is. Laila, this is your cousin, Dee, my sister Dorothy's child. And this is your other cousin, Clive, my brother Bob's boy. And this?"

Dee told him who Andy was. She knew the strange woman in black was being explained to her, but she had been too stunned to understand. Six of them packed into the big Chrysler, Andy driving. They'd dropped this stranger woman, this Pearl, at a blue house in Inglewood where the light was on over the door. Dee had not then, and scarcely since, the slightest idea who she was.

While they drove on, Jonas told the tale. He had married, he said, a woman, a French woman, in the islands years ago. Not until the February gone, Uncle Jonas said, had he known he had a daughter. The woman was then dying, and the word passed to him in some mysterious way. He had gone quickly and whisked his child out of that world, some tiny French island far, far in the western ocean and far under . . . and he had whisked her into this one. He had been carting her around the globe, for a treat, to get acquainted, Jonas said. It was a tale typical of Jonas. You believed it or not. He didn't care.

"She's seen a lot, you know," said he. "But, funny thing, seen the least of this country. Flew on from New York. I'm tired, Dee. We should have taken a train and stopped over and seen things. But I'm tired. Felt like getting home."

Dee remembered the stab of her premonition. Uncle Jonas had never said such a thing in his life, before.

The big shabby house tucked under the hills above Los Feliz had been blazing for them and Mrs. Vaughn beside herself with welcome. It had never seemed shabby before. Décor never mattered where Jonas was; he shed his own splendour. But the girl, the dainty lovely little female creature was not at home in the heavy mahogany, the rusty brocade.

Dee remembered the three of them driving away, later.

Clive, chewing his lip, had finally said what had been burning in his mind. "I suppose she *is* his daughter? I suppose he *did* get married?"

Dee herself had no illusions really. Jonas's goings-on had not always—or even after—been within the law, and he had not amassed his wealth by a sober attention to rules and regulations. Dee wondered, indulgently, how many women of how many colours Uncle Jonas might have married in how many islands. But she said staunchly, "Of course. Since he says so."

Andy said, "Your Uncle Jonas is a character, all right. I like him."

Dee, glad of that, pressing her cheek against his shoulder, said, "Ah, yes, . . . yes, he is. And she's a darling."

"Odd little thing. Exotic, eh?" Clive chewed it over.

Andy said with full enthusiasm, "And very charming."

* * *

The convertible was rolling swiftly up the high-gear road; it passed the Greek theatre, made the curve at the bird sanctuary.

Dee, in her mind's eye, saw the roll of three intervening months, and the charm of her little cousin Laila, as it had been revealed. Saw her at the beach, saw the slim, lithe body sliding and flashing in the water with her long black hair clinging and following, a sight as wondrous as a mermaid. Saw, in her mind's eye, Andy on the beach, watching under half-drawn lids, muting his enthusiasm, becoming wary of showing it, beginning to hide what he felt.

Laila was a child of the sea, at home there. But on land she was lost. Never been to school at all. Jonas agreed there must be tutors, soon. Couldn't send her to kindergarten at eighteen. Couldn't throw her in with a group her own age, not the weird mixture of knowledge and ignorance that she was. Been around the world, Egypt, Paris, London and Rome. But unable to drive a car, and scared of a telephone. Laila spoke French as well as she did English. Could just about write her name. Couldn't really read a newspaper. Could order in two languages from a menu card—the most expensive stuff. Didn't know the multiplication table or anything else about arithmetic or indeed any science. Lost in a world like this one.

But fascinating. All Dee's days were taken up in a strange duty to be cousin, friend, guide and counsellor to her little cousin, Laila Breen.

And yet, she thought, it wouldn't have been so bad, so totally disrupting, if Jonas hadn't had to die.

Jonas, of course, had known, and said *yes* to death,

just as he always had to life. His oldest friend, Dr. John Stirling, had been hopeful at the beginning. But Jonas grinned. "Don't kid me, John. You don't really know one damn thing about what ails me. All you've got is a name for it. So have I. Call it dying."

Nevertheless, Stirling had set himself to do battle. At the last, he had moved Jonas into his own small hospital. That was when Dee left her job and moved into the house. Had to. Couldn't leave Laila to the mercies of the servants. Or to those of Pearl Dean, who persisted, who came too often, whom Stirling detested, and Andy disliked, and Dee herself could not fathom. Nor leave the little cousin to her cousin Clive, either. Clive was . . . too rootless.

Anyhow, Jonas had said so. "Take care of the little one, Dee, and watch Clive, eh?"

"Oh, I will."

"Clive's not what I'd call responsible. Financially, for instance. Never takes a risk. Thinks he does. But that boy goes like an arrow to a *certain* loss." Jonas chuckled. "Some basic misunderstanding of the whole thing, Dee."

"I know."

"And Pearl Dean. Well, I'm fond of her, Dee, but she won't do for Laila. Takes a hard head, first. Then, you can enjoy Pearl Dean."

"Yes, Jonas, I know. I'll watch."

"Going to give Stirling the worst of the job. I like your young man, Dee."

"So do I, Jonas."

"He'll take care of *you*, my dearie. He'll make a good fight of it. Nothing would disappoint him like missing the battle . . ." Jonas sighed.

"I suppose not, Jonas."

"Take care of the little one, Dee. I want her to be a whole lot like you."

"Oh, Jonas, darling, don't you leave us."

"Expect I'll get along soon. See what's next, eh? Hold the fort, Dee." Dee's heart ached for him still.

No question, after that. Dee lived in the gloomy old mansion. It was her place. But her own life, just begun, had suffered a kind of cancellation.

The convertible reached the plateau at the observatory and hunted a parking space along the rail. The city was down there like a great living coloured map, and they could see the sea shine like a sliver of mirror far away.

Well, thought Dee, not resentfully, but numb before the facts, here on the top of this little mountain, is where I get my heart broken.

There were things that had not been said, as well she knew.

There was the day that Jonas died.

For once, that morning, Dee let Laila go with Pearl Dean, who would soothe her with cloudy sayings. The servants threw themselves into tasks. Lorraine, the capable and conscientious woman, pretended to be scandalized by the dusty books and made Sidney, her husband, lift them down while she scrubbed the shelves. In the kitchen, poor old Berta Vaughn, red-eyed too soon, comforted herself in her own way. She reverted that morning to her old solitary habit, although Jonas had forbidden her vegetable patch, and no more would her slight, energetic figure creep along the ground among the beets and the beans, or would she can and store and gloat over the long cellar shelves. Dee understood why Mrs. Vaughn was canning peaches that morning. Why the house smelled of sugar and spice. Why Lorraine attacked the shelves with such fury.

Dee herself would have been glad to pound a typewriter with somebody else's words, but she, uprooted from her own habits, could only flutter from library to kitchen, pretending to supervise, denying the doom of that miserable day. At noon, Clive called from the hospital.

Jonas was in a coma.

Dee saw herself at the hospital, struggling with sorrow, trying, in Stirling's office across the hall from where Jonas lay, to get a message to Andy. Vivid as yesterday, she saw herself giving up, and putting her foot into the hall, and seeing with a surge of thanks his tall figure against the light of the entrance lounge. Vivid as yesterday, she saw her little cousin come creeping out of Jonas's room, turn on her toe, fly toward the lounge, run bodily into Clive who was restlessly walking in the corridor. Clive said some sharp thing to her which seemed to send her ricocheting away from him into Andy's arms.

Vivid as yesterday, Dee saw him enfold her, saw his head bending, saw the exquisite tenderness with which her lover accepted the dark head of her cousin Laila against his breast.

Even now, the sight stabbed her.

She'd seen Laila pass on like a little cork, bobbing on down the corridor into the harbour of Pearl Dean's black crêpe bosom, and then Dee turned to face Dr. John in Jonas's door and the fact that Jonas was dead.

Andy had come up quietly behind her and stood by.

Nothing had ever been said.

But now he had something to say.

The convertible nosed the rail. Dee shifted the package beside her feet. "Why do you have to run errands?" Andy growled. "All those servants. All that money." He took out cigarettes and gave her one.

Andy was touchy about money. Dee remembered the evening after Jonas was dead, and Laila had been put to bed with what comfort Dee could give her. Downstairs, in Jonas's library, among the new-scrubbed shelves, Clive, who was spending the night at the house, had been mixing himself a drink. He said in his rather pleasant light tenor, "Look, do us grown-ups want to face facts? I can tell you what's in the will, if you want to know."

"I'd like to know," Andy admitted. He looked grim, and uneasy. "How do you know? Did Jonas tell you?"

"I happen to know," evaded Clive. "I think you should hear this, Dee. Jonas left you five thousand, and me the same." He grimaced. "So, Talbot, if you had any dream that Dee was an heiress, forget it. Laila gets half a million in trust. Stirling's her guardian."

"That's wise," Dee said.

"Is it?" Clive gulped his drink.

"Of course, she needs it. We don't."

"What do you mean we don't?" Clive bristled.

"She means," said Andy, his tension gone, "that we are equipped to earn our way. I, for one, would rather.

14

Whereas, Laila . . ."

"Eyewash," said Clive with a startled look. "Nobody would rather not have, say, a hundred grand. I think Jonas could have made a better division."

"Speak for yourself," Andy said coldly.

Clive had watched him over the glass. "You got a prejudice against marrying money?"

"Maybe," said Andy shortly. "My father married my stepmother for money. I saw what it did to him. Anyhow, I intend to get paid darned well for the work I do, and get a kick out of it."

Clive smiled in a patronizing sort of way. "Well, then, you are in love with your work, eh? Well, then, you've got no problems."

Andy said, too angrily, "You think there's only one. How to get money for nothing."

Dee remembered the disproportionate anger, then Andy's struggle to control it. Andy had gone home rather abruptly after that.

"He's got problems, Dee," Clive had said when Andy was gone.

"I'm going up, Clive. I'm tired."

"Me too, soon. Listen, Dee . . . I was close enough to them, down there today, to hear. Do you want to know what was said?"

"No, thank you."

Clive paid no attention. "Laila says, 'Oh Andrew, take me away! Take me away from here!' And your boy, Talbot, *he* says, 'I can't. There's Dee.' " Then Clive had stood watching her with his light eyes, poised and urbane in his well-cut suit, the glass easy in his hand. "So don't kid yourself, Dee. He's got problems."

Dee had held herself quite steady. "Good night,

Clive. Don't drink the whole bottle."

"I don't drink, Dee. I'm no lush. You're just annoyed. But it's a tip, that's all. Better get back to that office, hadn't you? I'll keep an eye on Laila. Be glad to. I mean, you're in love with this guy, Talbot, aren't you? You better watch it."

She'd walked away and up the stairs and seen his sleek head turn carelessly away.

She said, aloud, "What is it, Andy? What did you want to say?"

He twisted and faced her. "How long are you going to take, raising your little cousin Laila?"

"It takes time," she gasped.

"Get Dr. Stirling to fix her up in some school, Dee."

"How can he?"

"She'll study alone." Impatience crept into his voice. "And you'll have to live there. How long?"

"I don't know. I can't leave her. I'm the only girl she knows to speak to in this entire hemisphere."

"That's wrong."

"I know it's wrong. But it takes time. We've been grieving . . ."

"Ah, Dee, can't you see? It isn't only schooling. It's everything. You're not the one to teach her all she's got to learn. You're only twenty-one, yourself. You're not even the type."

"I never wanted to be a teacher," she confessed.

"Dr. Stirling has got to let you off this job. If you won't tell him so, I will."

"Don't do that, Andy. It *is* my job."

"Not so. He's her legal guardian. It's up to him. There's plenty of money. He can hire it done."

"It's not easy," murmured Dee. "Laila at least feels trusting toward me. Dr. John seems to frighten her. I don't."

"Why does it fall on you?" he said, stubbornly. "What about Clive, who is equally her cousin? What about that Pearl Dean who says she was a friend of Laila's mother, or something like that?"

Dee stiffened. "I'd just as soon throw the poor child to a pack of wolves. No, I'm to take care of her. Jonas asked me to. I can't help it, Andy. There it is."

"You won't concede there comes a time to turn things over to other people?"

"You don't give up in the middle," Dee said hotly. "You can't just stop and say 'I'm through.'"

"Well, then," he said, sinking back, "there it is. You're proud, Dee. You're reckless, too." His face brooded, the argument lost, the vehemence gone.

"I don't see how . . ." she faltered.

"Yes, you do. You must know Laila's taken quite a lively fancy to . . . me."

"Perhaps," said Dee faintly.

"Not her fault," he said, looking white around the mouth. "I'm the only youngish man she knows, to speak to, in this hemisphere, not counting Clive. Dee, won't you look at it from where I sit? I can't see you at the office. You're never there. I come to the house. There's Laila. I take a day off, try to fix it so we get one Wednesday afternoon. But Laila's coming, too."

"You don't dislike her," Dee said, a trifle bitterly.

"No," he said soberly. "Maybe I better tell you this. Teaching may not appeal to you. It appeals to me."

"What do you mean, Andy?" Dee's heart jumped.

"It's an attraction," he said. His face was sombre and he looked off at the sky. "A man almost can't stand

17

not to take that girl in his hands and mould her into what he'd like a girl to be. Maybe you don't understand that."

"I do understand that," Dee said gravely, proudly.

"Then will you please tell Stirling the job's too much for you, which it is. . . ."

"I can't." Her fists were clenched in her lap.

He brought his own clenched fist down on the steering wheel. "You don't like to admit anything's too much for you, do you, ma'am?"

She said, "I have to do this, Andy, the best I can."

"Drop it, Dee." His voice shook a little. "Walk out on it. I'm begging you . . ."

"I can't walk out on her," said Dee sadly, "until she's . . . raised, as you say." Her heart flopped. Her head tilted proudly. "Unless someone I admired and trusted were to take the job. Unless . . . you took it, Andy. You can teach her, if you like. Jonas approved of you, and it's a free country."

He turned the sharp silver of his eyes. "No, I cannot," he said furiously. "Do you think I'm going to take advantage of a childish crush? What do you think I'm going to do? Throw you over and marry half a million dollars?"

"Whatever I think," said Dee steadily, "it isn't that. I just think she's . . . very attractive."

"You make it tough," he said, and stared at the view.

"I don't find it easy. I'm jealous, sometimes. But I love the little thing, Andy; that's a part of it. And she is my job. Jonas said so. How can I do anything else but what I'm doing?"

"I don't suppose you can," he said slowly. "Not even to help me. So I do this alone. Well," he murmured, "it's a free country."

18

"Yes," she said proudly, "that it is."

"All right. I'm just giving notice, Dee," he told her, still staring at the sky, "that until something happens to break up this weird triangle where everybody loves everybody else, I won't marry you. I won't move in there."

"I don't suppose you can," she agreed sadly.

He slammed the car into motion and whipped it backwards. They rolled off the plateau, down around the mountain, through the tunnel, back on down.

"Free country," Andy murmured. "Everyone does what he thinks is best and takes the consequences. Not so?"

"That's so, I guess," Dee said.

Chapter Two

Uncle Jonas Breen's big yellow stucco house was almost invisible from the street, all choked away by the wild growth of neglect. The car burrowed into the semi-circular driveway and only as it rolled before the portico, where the paint peeled, could they see a shabby little coupé pulled up behind a black sedan.

"La Pearl," said Andy grimly. "*And* Dr. Stirling. What do you want to bet? Complications!"

"Do you suppose somebody's ill?" Dee flashed out of the car and up to the door.

Lorraine, the housemaid, who opened it as if she had been waiting behind it, was a large woman who carried herself high. Now she seemed on tiptoe with tension.

"Oh, Miss Dee, I'm glad you're back. It's Mrs. Vaughn."

"What's the matter?"

"There's something wrong with her eyes."

"Eyes!"

"She doesn't feel a bit well. Been lying down. Maybe it's nothing but I finally . . . I hope I was right, Miss Dee . . . I called Dr. Stirling."

"You did just right, Lorraine," said Dee warmly. "Where's Miss Laila?"

"In there." Lorraine made a backward movement of her head. "Miss Pearl Dean is with her. They just came in a few . . ."

"Do they know Mrs. Vaughn isn't well?"

"Oh yes, Miss Dee, but Dr. Stirling" . . . Lorraine looked worried . . . "wouldn't let them near her."

It crossed Dee's mind that perhaps whatever ailed the housekeeper was contagious. "All right, Lorraine."

"Oh, Dee?" said the sweet high voice of her cousin Laila. Dee felt, almost physically, the darling burden fastening down upon her.

"I'll come in a minute." Dee nodded at the maid and moved across the wide entrance hall toward the big room at the left. She thought again that she must confer with Dr. Stirling about this place, about chopping the muffling shrubbery ruthlessly away, about new colour on the dull walls, and the dark massive furniture, about new light and new grace to be let in here somehow.

It took time.

Laila came dancing across the sombre rug. "I've been out with Pearl. To lunch. Wasn't it kind of her, Dee?"

"Hi, sweetie," said Dee with a melting heart. The child was so easily, so pathetically delighted by anyone's kindness. "Why aren't you wearing something cooler, you little goose?"

All the way around the world with Uncle Jonas, Laila had worn a tailored suit, as was proper for a traveller. Now she seemed to think it was the only proper garment, although her lithe little body denied the whole idea of formality, and her long dark hair that never seemed to need a ribbon or a pin to keep it away from her flower face was a shock of loveliness and incongruity. She was all contradictions. Her feet that somehow ought to have been bare were in nylons and pumps. Her hands, that now reached for Dee in affection, were tough calloused little hands.

Laila was altogether a tougher little body than she appeared. It's her spirit, thought Dee, that is frail and defenceless.

"Coolness," said Pearl Dean in her soft booming voice, "is only an attitude. Are you well, Dee?"

"I'm well. And you?" said Dee mechanically. She was watching Laila's face transformed with radiant surprise.

"Oh, Andrew!" The little girl clasped her hands as if the sight of him was a gift. It was innocent. It was lovely. It was appealing.

"Hiya, Laila." Andy came up behind. "Pearl?" He bowed and there was mockery in the bow. "Are you well?" he inquired.

"I am always well," said Pearl, rolling her great cow eyes. "I am leaving now."

Andy said, "Good. Excuse me, Pearl. We are going to the beach. If you are leaving, then Laila can come along. I'll wait."

He walked past the girl and Pearl Dean and pushed through a glass door out into the patio.

The effect was a little rude, a little arrogant. But Dee knew he did it because of the churning turbulence of his mood. She stood still and forgave him and understood him — and watched her cousin Laila go dancing after him as if she were a little toy with wheels drawn by a string at his heels. She met the liquid roll of Pearl Dean's remarkable eyes.

The woman stood with her fat heels planted. The lank drab hair, cut short, grew sparsely from her big skull from which the dome of her abnormally high forehead shone forth like marble. La Pearl was a great one for intuitions. Dee wondered whether the woman could divine how often Dee had discussed with Dr. Stirling the problem of weaning Laila away from her peculiar influence.

"Andrew Talbot is not right for her, you know," said Pearl with her insufferable air of having been told these things by invisible angels.

Dee said sharply, "What do you mean?"

"They must not marry."

"Since he is engaged to marry *me*," said Dee flushing, "you're not very flattering, Pearl."

"Oh, time," said Pearl in her grand manner, "corrodes a promise. He is too old for her, too cold, too dedicated to the brain."

Dee winced. Pay no attention, she told herself sternly, don't bother to get mad.

"It's a free country," she said airily. "If you'll excuse me . . ."

Pearl took a step and grasped Dee by the wrist.

"She must have young love, Dee. The sun and the sea are well enough but love is her food. She can die without it."

"I hope she'll have it," said Dee politely. She couldn't follow. She never quite knew what Pearl Dean was talking about.

"I feel danger, like an evil perfume, all around her."

The woman moved still closer. The mass of her body was overpowering.

"Danger?" said Dee numbly.

"Yes, danger. Dee, I am a gypsy, as you know. Soon I shall run away from this city. Let me take her."

"Pearl, I can't."

"But Jonas knows I love her. Jonas understands. Dee, I could protect her. Dee, I must have her. Laila would be happy."

For a moment, Dee could see the two of them rocketing off, living on the fringe of the solid world, eating herbs, worshipping the sun. Oh yes, Laila would be happy enough. And Laila would be — somewhere else.

She said quietly, "Jonas didn't say you could have her, Pearl. I'm sorry. And I don't know what you mean by danger."

Pearl Dean dropped Dee's wrist as if she flung it down.

"Why is Dr. Stirling Laila's guardian?"

"Because Jonas said so," said Dee, shortly. As usual, she was being reduced to bluntness with this woman.

"Jonas has no faith in doctors. I cannot understand his faith in that man."

"That man was his oldest friend," Dee said. She resented Pearl's use of the present tense. Jonas was *not* present. She wished he were, but he was dead.

"Ah," said Pearl, "but each chooses his illusion and there is a V in time. Jonas Breen is a man of wisdom. So mellow and wise. And open-minded." The great eyes rolled. "He and John Stirling are poles apart." She held her plump hands apart to illustrate.

"Pearl," said Dee wearily, "there are some kinds of wisdom —" She took a break. "Do you know what crosses my mind about you sometimes?" The woman simply waited. "Whether you ever knew Laila's mother at all. Or whether you just picked up Jonas and his daughter on shipboard three months ago."

The woman's quick intuition flew to the point. "Because he was rich, you think? Yes. That is the superstition. But I don't care for money. I am not possessed. I have the sun and sky and the gift of wonder. And so does Jonas Breen for all his prosperity. We must not quarrel, Dee, you and I." The big voice purred. "I don't think *you* care for money. I think you care for And—"

"Why, I like it fine," said Dee flippantly. "Very pleasant stuff, money. What's the matter with it?" She grinned at the woman.

"You are saucy," said Pearl, "but I will tell you something. If Andrew Talbot were not afraid of money, if money were merely pleasant stuff to *him*, instead of standing in his heart's way—"

"I don't think his heart is your business," Dee flared and then snatched at her temper. "Pearl, I don't want to quarrel with you, either, but it's the dickens of an effort sometimes. Andy isn't your business and neither, I'm sorry to have to say so bluntly, is Laila."

Pearl had closed her eyes. "For your own sake, you should let her go. You are blind when you will not see," she intoned.

"You haven't answered me," said Dee sharply. "*Did* you know Laila's mother?"

The white eyelids trembled. "In a way you would not understand. In another world."

"I thought so," said Dee flatly, "but not in this world. And Jonas left her in this plain world that we see, Pearl. So you can't have her. And—will you please excuse me. Mrs. Vaughn is ill . . ."

Then Pearl's eyes came wide open like oysters in her heavy face. "I could have helped poor Berta Vaughn," she said contemptuously, "if your Dr. Stirling were not such a narrow man. You disappoint me, Dee. You don't trust me? You think the world's so plain? Very well, I am leaving." Without turning her head, Pearl called "Laila?"

Dee heard Laila answer, saw her come in from the

25

outer air to this gloomy room. She didn't like the obedience, the reverence and trust.

"You will see me on my way?" said Pearl.

"Yes, Pearl."

Pearl touched her, like a benediction. "You will take
strength from the sun and the sea and the blessed
wind, little darling?"

"Yes, Pearl."

"You will be happy."

"Yes, Pearl."

"Come." Pearl's ponderous figure began her waddle
to the door and Laila went after.

Oh, thought Dee, anyone can lead her. Anyone can
teach her. Anyone who wants to try. *That's* dangerous.

She whirled round. By the tall clock, it was a little
after one. Things for Dee to do. See about the ailing
housekeeper. Talk to the doctor. And somehow *do*
something about Pearl Dean.

Then she saw Andy, standing against the light in
the narrow french window, and for one quivering moment they looked at each other. He seemed to be saying, "See what I mean?"

Dee thought defiantly, But I am responsible.

Dr. John Stirling's rasping querulous voice came
ahead of him out of the pantry. "Carelessness. Ignorance. Absolutely unnecessary." He came fuming. He
glared at Dee as was his custom. "Tell you in a minute, Dee," he said. "Got to phone for the ambulance."

Dee stepped backwards and touched her hand to the
wall. Whatever ailed Mrs. Vaughn, it was not "nothing". Dee must go to her at once.

She heard the doctor bark some medical terms into
the phone. She heard him say, "No, too late for that.
Symptoms are violent already. Get the ambulance

along and take over as soon as they bring her in. . . .
No, I'll be along later. I've got to find it."

Find what, Dee wondered?

She look up the chair. "I won't
Dee, I don't especially want to talk to you. I'm
tired."

Chapter Three

Old Mrs. Vaughn lay on the coverlet with her eyes
shut.

"Are you in pain, Mrs. Vaughn?"

The woman couldn't seem to swallow or bring herself to speak. Her eyes opened but they were queer
and wild. Dee put her hand on the crumpled skin of
the cheek and the pale forehead. It did not seem to
her to be feverish at all. She looked around at Lorraine. "When did she begin to feel ill?"

"The middle of the morning, Miss Dee. It was her
eyes."

"Eyes," Dee shook her head. There was nothing she
could do here. "I think the doctor has called an ambulance. I'd better talk to him. You'll stay?" Lorraine
nodded and Dee withdrew softly. She started back
through the kitchen and at the pantry door she met
the doctor.

"Dr. John, what is it? What can we do?"

"Hospital's the place for her," he barked. "Get the
phone, Dee."

"Oh?"

"Clive," he said. "You talk to him."

So Dee went through the pantry, walking like an au-
tomaton. Yes, take the phone call. The day was broken into pieces. She no longer knew what was going to
become of it. No one was there in the gloomy hall.

She took up the phone. "Clive?"

"Dee? I didn't especially want to talk to you, Dee. Where's Laila?"

"What do you want with Laila?"

"I want to talk to her, naturally." Clive's voice was unfriendly on the wire.

"What's happened now," said Dee patiently, "that you need money for?"

"All right, listen, girl scout. They just repossessed my car."

"Too bad."

"Too bad! It's outrageous! A lousy two hundred dollars. Listen, Dee, how about you? I'd . . ."

"Not me," said Dee crisply. "Not Laila, either."

"Dee," said her cousin Clive, "what's the matter you? You're getting to sound more and more like an old-maid chaperone. Listen, if Laila's got a little milk of human kindness in her, I can't see what business it is of yours. She'd lend me two hundred dollars, if you'd let her alone. Now let me talk to her, will you?"

Clive was wound up in his own troubles.

"She's out saying good-bye to Pearl Dean at the moment. I'll advise her not to lend you anything, Clive. You might as well . . ."

"I'm coming up there."

"Well, I can't stop you," said Dee wearily, and hung up.

She wondered how Clive had managed to get rid of his legacy so soon, before it had even come physically into his hands. She knew he had. She thought for a moment, rebelliously, that she was tired of sounding like an old-maid chaperone. Maybe she ought to let Laila do as she would impulsively please. Laila had a frightening bank account. She didn't know how to spend money. It was one more thing to teach her.

Dee sighed and stepped to the house door, and there was Laila. "Clive's coming up. He wants you to lend him some more money." Dee watched her cousin.

"Oh, does he need it?" said Laila.

"He always needs it. Sweetie, you shouldn't do it."

"Shouldn't I?" Dee saw the look of obedience, of reverence, and she wished it were not worn for her, either.

"Think about it," she urged. "You've loaned him a lot already and he hasn't even tried to pay it back. You'd be giving it to him, sweetie."

"But shouldn't I, Dee?"

"It . . . just isn't very good for him." Dee suddenly gave it up. "Never mind. You do what you want," she said gently. "Look, sweetie, we may not get to go to the beach after all. Poor Mrs. Vaughn is quite ill, I guess."

"I know," said Laila. "I'm so sorry. But Dr. John sent me away from her. He sent Pearl away, Dee. Pearl could have helped her."

The girl's eyes, so full of trust, were asking Dee to explain? How could she tell her that Pearl Dean had seceded from the common experience of western man and was, instead, a healer on some mystical basis invented by herself. Dee had tried to keep an open mind. She knew many earnest people were looking for clues in some odd but not necessarily unfruitful directions. But Pearl Dean repudiated all these, too. The monstrous egoism was repelling.

Now, she said gently, "Do you think so, Laila?" For how could she explain?

"But Dee, of course. She helps everyone. She helps me."

"Sweetie, you never feel ill, do you?"

"No, never," said Laila, rising on her toes as if she would leave the earth and fly. "I feel wonderful, always. Pearl does, too. It is easy to be well, Dee."

"But if you ever feel—not altogether well, you must tell me, sweetie. Or tell Dr. John."

The girl's eyes flashed. It was a look of fear.

Dee said, "You know, Jonas wanted Dr. John and me to take care of you."

"You'll take care of me, Dee," said Laila, "until I understand better." Her eyes were clear as spring water dyed leaf-brown.

"Of course," Dee hugged her shoulders. "I must talk to the doctor. Maybe we can go. I'll see."

"I hope we can go," said Laila. "Where is Andrew? Oh, I do love"—her breath caught—"to be at the beach, Dee."

"I know you do," said Dee.

She turned away. She knew Laila went flying across the dim sitting-room to the glass doors and out to the patio, the one open and airy spot, saved from the encroachment of greenery by having been firmly paved long ago. Dee thought, she could have a swimming-pool out there where Mrs. Vaughn's vegetable patch is going to seed. There's plenty of money. I must see about it. I must get her away from that Pearl. The tutor must come soon. I sound like her grandmother.

She came into the kitchen. From the high windows that overlooked the patio, she could see Andy standing with his hands in his blue denim pockets staring down at the broken fountain. She saw Laila whirl gracefully to sit on the tiled rim and look up with adoration into his face.

Dee opened her clenched hands. She thought, well

if he loves her, why, then, he does.

Dr. Stirling had the refrigerator open and was rooting around inside of it.

"Dee," he said sharply. "Come here."

"Yes, Doctor?"

"What have you eaten out of this lot?"

Startled, she moved to look past his shoulder. "Eaten of, you mean? Not much. The ham was last night's dinner. Lettuce, of course. Butter."

"This, too?" He was peering at a glass-covered dish.

"No, we had spinach with the ham, of course. It's a law."

"Lunch here today, Dee?" His voice was muffled. He didn't respond to her little joke.

"Not I," she said. "I was shopping. Andy picked me up and we had a bite, just now."

He grunted. "Call Lorraine a minute, will you?"

When Lorraine came he had the glass dish on the sink and the cover off. "Lorraine, did you eat any of this stuff? Salad, isn't it?"

"No, sir."

"When was it made?"

"Yesterday, I believe, sir. Mrs. Vaughn must have made it yesterday noon."

"And she ate it *then?*" Dr. Stirling asked questions for the sake of getting answers. He had a buzz in his voice and was as concentrated and tactless as a bee.

"I guess she did," said Lorraine, sounding frightened and defensive. "I was off for the afternoon. I wasn't here."

"What is it, Dr. John?" Dee felt frightened, too. "What ails her?"

"I'm guessing," he buzzed, "but I'm guessing good Dee, and I don't like what I'm guessing. Um. Who

32

else ate this stuff? That chauffeur fellow, your husband?"

Lorraine said, "Oh no, I don't think so, sir. He was off with me yesterday and anyhow, he won't touch a cold salad. Never would."

The doctor's rough grey head came up sharply. "How about Laila? Did she eat any of this?"

"Not yesterday," said Dee quickly, "because she went with me to the tennis matches. We lunched near there."

"What about today?"

Lorraine said, quavering, "I don't know, sir. Miss Dean came and took her away, about eleven-thirty it was."

"That's right," Dee said, her blood tingling with relief. "They lunched together. She told me."

"Out? In a restaurant? Not here?"

"Not here," said Lorraine, "because Mrs. Vaughn was sick and I never did make any lunch today. I haven't even had any."

The doctor grunted. "Lucky for you, you haven't. Nobody ate of this but Mrs. Vaughn herself. Um-hum."

"You think there is something wrong with it, Dr. John?"

"I sure do, Dee. String-bean salad. Now, I'll bet," the doctor raised again his tousled head, "these beans came from a can."

"No, sir. From a glass jar," said Lorraine shakily.

"Home canned?" he pounced.

"Mrs. Vaughn canned them. Yes, sir. Out of her garden. She's canned lots of stuff. It was kind of her hobby while the house was closed."

The doctor fixed her with a stern eye. "And she took

33

the cold beans out of the jar and put the salad dressing on them?"

"Yes, sir."

"She didn't boil them?"

"I don't think so, sir. I've seen her do that. What you said."

"May not be conclusive," said the doctor, "but it's good enough for me to go on. All right," he snapped. "Where do you keep that canned stuff?"

"In the cellar."

"Locked?"

"Yes, it's locked, sir."

"Make sure it's locked now, and bring me the key."

"Yes, sir." Lorraine went dithering away.

"Can't have the whole lot of you poisoned," the doctor said.

"Poisoned! The whole cellar! Dr. John, what do you mean?"

"I mean *Bacillus botulinus,* and that's a cute little poison, believe me."

Dee heard a soft whistle and turned. Andy was standing, alone, in the pantry door, with his face sober.

The doctor was hunting the kitchen drawers. "Wrapping-paper," he demanded. "Hello, Talbot."

Dee moved to show him where the wrapping-paper was. Fragments of knowledge were coming into her mind. She heard Andy say, as if he knew, "That's bad, eh?"

"How bad is it?" she asked quietly.

The doctor shot a sharp look at her. "You should never . . ." he began in his exasperated rasp. "Well, the old lady didn't know, or if she knew, she forgot. But she ought to have known. Even if the toxin forms, you can kill it by six minutes of boiling. Looks like she didn't do that. All I can say, it's lucky the whole household wasn't bowled over."

"Dr. John," said Dee forcefully, "you'd better tell me. Do people die?"

He said, "Yes, people die."

"Oh!" It was Lorraine, who cried out sharply. She put the key on the sink and cried, "Sidney! He's at the garage getting the car fixed! I don't know the name of it! Oh, Miss Dee, I got to go there! I got to see if he's all right."

"Of course you do," said Dee quickly.

"Now, now," said the doctor briskly, "they don't *always* die." But Lorraine had gone, stumbling out the back way.

Andy was saying, "Isn't there such as a thing as an antitoxin?"

And Stirling answered, "Yes, there is. But the trouble with that is, by the time you can diagnose this stuff, it's too late. Still . . . one thing and another . . . we can try. Depends on how much she got. Listen, hear it?"

"Ambulance," said Andy.

"Dee, see if the old lady's ready."

"Where's Laila?" Dee turned her head to look back.

Andy said, "Laila's upstairs. Better she stays there." She felt her heart buckle, as if it would soon break, so sad and so tender was his voice upon her cousin's name.

Chapter Four

When the bustle was over, the stricken housekeeper had been carried off to Dr. Stirling's hospital, and the doctor had gone, too, after many warnings, but with the bean salad wrapped beside him on the seat of his car, then Dee sat down.

She sat on the stairs. The hall clock said one-thirty-five. The sun was blazing on the sand, somewhere.

Dee was thinking. Ignorance. Poor old Mrs. Vaughn may have destroyed herself, in ignorance. How could Dee keep her little ignorant cousin safe? Pearl was right! Laila was in danger! Traffic. That alone! And electricity. Not to touch with a wet hand. Fuses and all of that. And gas. Carbon monoxide. And all the drugs and poisons blithely used. How to teach her about the daily dangers so close and familiar that they are avoided without thought?

She said aloud, "How can I even tell her what *happened* to Mrs. Vaughn?"

"Laila?" said Andy. He was standing there at the newel post and looking past her up the stairs.

"It's going to sound to her like magic sounds to me." Dee thought of the whole generations of experiment, study, and slow gain that lay behind the doctor's diagnosis.

"Tell her it was an evil spirit in the beans," said Andy grimly. "Will you want to go down to the hospital?"

"Yes, I think I—"

"Ought," he finished. But he touched her shoulder. "Dee, don't be so upset. The poor old soul could have done this any day in the last twenty years."

"Andy, where is Laila? Did she go up to change?"

He hesitated, so long that Dee looked up at him.

"She . . . wouldn't be going to the beach with us," he said at last.

"Why not?"

He sat down on the carpet-covered stairs beside her.

"Matter of fact, I took the opportunity. I warned you, Dee."

"You . . . warned me!"

"I pointed out a few things to Laila. I told her, for one thing, how much you were giving up to stay here and take care of her."

Dee had the feeling that sometimes comes to a redhead, of bursting into flames at the top.

"And I told her, further, that since I am engaged to you," said Andy bleakly, "she had better put out of her head any tender thoughts. I told her . . . they were getting to be a nuisance to both of us."

"Oh, Andy . . ." Dee's anger broke into dismay.

His face was stubborn. "Dee, we were getting all snarled up in a pretty uncomfortable state of affairs. Now you're thinking how cruel I was. You're wrong, Dee. It took a little nerve."

"To break her heart! I should think it might."

"She's too young to have her heart broken," he said with that bleak expression. "Be more like a greenstick fracture. I was as gentle as I could be."

Dee said slowly, "You did what you thought was best and it's a free country."

"Exactly."

"You were *wrong!*" Dee blazed.

He leaned away from her . . . more than his body withdrew. He looked at her from afar. "How so?" he asked remotely

"Do you think I'm going to take advantage of a . . . a promise? Do you think I'm going to marry a man about half in love with another girl?"

"All right Dee," he said, helplessly.

"You don't deny it?"

"No, I don't deny it." His eyes were honest. "I was trying . . ."

"Don't *try.*" She stripped his ring from her finger and his hand came up and received it. He started to speak but she went on: "You can't pretend. You can't start your life on a . . . a noble resolution. Andy, let me tell you something. Maybe you don't think I know. I *look* pretty startling. You say I blind. All right. I know that. I've had to cope with it all my life. Because my hair's so red, my eyes so blue. I've got good legs and my nose is straight. People are startled. Up till now I've always made a discount for that. But I fell in love with you and so I forgot. But it's possible, now that you're used to the razzle-dazzle, you don't even like me. I'm no teacher. I'm too stubborn to be taught. Maybe there's not the attraction you expected. All right. You think better of it. I told you it's a free country."

"Dee," he said, "don't . . ."

"You said," she went on passionately, "you wouldn't marry me until this weird triangle was broken. Well, you can't break it by a resolution or an act of will.

38

And I don't . . . want it that way."

"All right, Dee," he said, again. "Now I think it's best if I disappear." He stood up. "I agree. I was wrong."

She gave him a look, wild with dismay.

"And I'll take the consequence," she cried. "Why didn't you tell me what you planned to do? You didn't break the impasse. You broke something else. I was her friend. She knew she could count on me. Now she won't dare feel the same. You've made her feel guilty about me. You had no business . . ."

"She'll have to learn to think sometime," he muttered. "She can't run forever on ignorance and feeling."

Dee covered her face.

There were rapid footsteps below and behind them. The pantry door was slapped open. Lorraine came rushing along. Her husband, Sidney Dickett, loomed behind her.

"Are you all right, Sidney?" said Dee at once. She pulled herself to her feet and leaned over the banister.

Lorraine was gasping for breath and could not find enough to speak but the man spoke. He was a bulky, a shambling man. Now his voice was incisive with alarm. "Lorraine says we got to tell you right away. I saw Miss Laila eating that stuff this morning."

"You . . . did?" Dee's hands on the banister were cold.

"Yeah. I went through the kitchen about eleven o'clock on my way to take the car down and she was standing by the sink and she had a plate of it and bread and butter."

"Are you . . . sure?"

"Bean salad," Sidney said. "It looked terrible. Beans

and goop. It musta been the same stuff."

"I suppose it must have been." A frightened note was creeping into Dee's voice.

"Wait a minute," said Andy quickly. "Watch out, now, Dee. Be careful. Laila won't understand it, you know. We'll have to get her to the hospital, I suppose, where Stirling can handle her."

"She's never been there," Dee murmured, "but once, the day Jonas died. She won't go any more."

"She's afraid?" Andy was alert. His hands gripped her shoulders. The stormy passage between them was forgotten.

"Yes, she's afraid," Dee said.

"Influence of La Pearl?"

"And Jonas, too. Jonas got into the hands of some quack once." Why are we standing here chattering, Dee thought.

"Shall I call Stirling, Dee?" Andy was speaking firmly and quietly.

Dee looked around. "I will. I will. Lorraine, you go up and just . . . just be with her. Don't say anything until I come. Just see if she's all right. Tell her about Mrs. Vaughn some . . . comforting way." The big woman nodded. There was no panic, only the strong sense of a need to act.

"I haven't got the car," Sidney said. "It's up on blocks."

"I've got mine," said Andy.

Dee was at the phone.

"When did she eat it and how much?" There was no change whatsoever in the quality of Dr. Stirling's rasp.

"This morning about eleven o'clock. I don't know how much. Sidney saw her. I suppose Lorraine was with Mrs. Vaughn and she was hungry."

"Take it easy, Dee. Remember I told you there is an antitoxin. Now this is what will happen." He was so matter-of-fact that Dee's hands began to relax. "We'll get hold of that. The symptoms of this damn stuff don't show up at all for from sixteen to thirty-six hours. D'you see? Now, if in that time we shoot the antitoxin to her, it'll be easy. So don't worry. Darn lucky for Laila we know what she got and know it so early. There's time, Dee. Now you just run her right down here, and everything's going to be O.K."

"You've got something that will s—stop it? You really have!"

"Certainly. So take it easy, mind, and get her down here."

"We will. We will."

"What does he say?" Andy demanded.

Dee told him.

"Then so long as she gets the antitoxin before too many hours, she's not in danger at all?"

"That's what he says!"

"Well, thank God," said Andy reverently. "Ain't science wonderful!" A weak smile went between them.

"She isn't there," said Lorraine.

Lorraine was halfway down the stairs.

"She isn't there?" Dee said stupidly. "She must have come down, then."

"Look out on the patio," said Andy. "Maybe the library . . ." He hurried across the rugs.

Sidney said, "Not there."

"Did you look in my room, Lorraine?" Dee began to run upstairs.

"Everywhere upstairs, Miss Dee. She's not up there."

Sidney ran outdoors to thrash about in the jungle of

41

the grounds. Dee turned on the stairs. Her body wanted to run very fast, somewhere. But her mind put the brakes on, asking where she must run. In that suspension she looked down and saw that Andy had come back. The skin of his face was an odd colour.

He said, "Maybe she ran away."

"Ran away?"

His voice was staccato.

"Because she'd had her heart broken."

Dee knew that this was so. She seemed to herself to be walking on eggshells. She took a step down.

"Was there anything," she asked him quietly, "to make you think she might?"

He moistened his lips. "She did say she wanted to be by herself. She ran into the house . . ."

"To be by herself," Dee repeated.

"Away from *me*. And you, I suppose. I suppose you were right."

Dee said, very quietly: "She's so young and I suppose she *felt* like running away. I suppose she runs on feeling, just as you said. I suppose that's it."

He didn't answer. He looked stricken.

Lorraine had collapsed on the stairs behind them. "Will she get like Mrs. Vaughn?" she moaned. "Poor sweet little thing! She will die?"

"Oh, no, of course not," said Dee vigorously. "We — we must just — find her."

"How many hours?" said Andy loudly.

"Sixteen —"

"Counting from — this morning?"

"Yes. Yes."

"Midnight, to be safe," he said. "Midnight. I'll find her."

Dee herself began to glow. It was an illusion caused

by determination. "We'll go, right now, and find her," Dee said.

"Wait a minute . . ." said Andy. "Use our heads. Need all the help we can get. She's got to be found." He ran to the phone.

Chapter Five

Laila Breen walked very fast. She thought she had better not run, although she wanted to. She walked down the curving, descending street, finding the heels of her pumps a nuisance and hating the clatter they made on the pavement. To be barefoot and running swiftly would be better. But she thought it might make people stare.

The sun and shadow through which she passed was all grey to her. She didn't want to be seen. She'd had a bad shock and her face felt hot with shame.

It hurt to look back and see and hear herself. She should have been sly. It would have been bitter-sweet to worship Andrew secretly and never let anyone notice. Then she could have loved him all her life. And when he and Dee were married, still keep the sweet bitterness, the darling pain.

Not now. No more.

And Dee would know everything. The wonderful, brilliant competence of Dee was something Laila admired. Still, it couldn't be borne if Dee knew everything. It was very easy to see, now, that she couldn't take so much from Dee, now that she had been told. She would be ashamed in front of Dee because it was Andrew who had to tell her.

Her heart felt sore about Dee — about Andrew.

Dee was one of the only three in the world whom

Laila had truly trusted. But that very trust was too much, Andrew said, to put on Dee and so it couldn't be any more.

There was only one person left, really.

Not Dee—not Andrew. No more.

Not Dr. Stirling. He always said "Nonsense!" But Jonas was dead, just the same.

Laila wished she were home, but there was no home. The old station was sold, her mother's things all gone to the four winds, the old life never to be again. It had been a house of women, since Laila could remember, her French grandfather dead before she was born.

Her American grandmother, for whose sake English was the tongue of the house, her mamma, herself. A home of dreaming women. Grandmother dreaming of old times, Mamma dreaming of a day to come, Laila tucked sweetly into a golden present tense, half dream. Grandmother for ever saying, "Emily, you should have gone with him. You should soon go to America." Mamma for ever replying, "And will *you* go?" "No." "Well, then." It was a refrain. It was like music. When Grandmother was gone, the refrain was silent. But when Mamma was gone, Jonas had been, and for Laila to come to America rang like an old chord, a sweet and familiar sound in her ear.

But now she wished she were home, and there was no home. There was nothing like it. No long days when Mamma sang and told her dreams or long slow nights listening to the sea and nobody telling time. There was only one link left to the kind of world it had been and that was Pearl Dean.

Pearl never said "Nonsense." Pearl had dreams. Pearl would understand.

45

Her heels hit the hard pavement noisily. She could hear a rush of traffic now somewhere beyond the trees.

She had no mother and no father and almost nobody, now. Jonas who had been so kind and loving, whom she had trusted totally, was dead, and she herself had seen it and never told anyone. Seen Dr. Stirling seize the cloth roughly and bare the skin and plunge in the wicked needle and press the shining cylinder close. The nurse had seen it, too, and pressed her stern lips together and a look had gone between them.

Neither had known Laila was there in that room, frightened and quiet as a bug. Neither had seen her slip away. Neither had ever mentioned that awful thing they'd done.

She had mentioned it only once. She'd run into cousin Clive and cried in her terror, "They're killing Jonas."

But Clive had told her sharply, "You mustn't *say* a thing like that, you little dope. That's libel. They could put you in *jail*, lock you up for that."

So she had *not* said it, ever again. But just the same, Jonas was dead.

All they told her was the news. Maybe she didn't understand! She was afraid to ask, but she didn't trust Dr. Stirling very much. She couldn't.

Anyhow Pearl said Jonas was gone away, not far, and only because he was needed in another world. It must be true.

There really wasn't anyone left in the whole world to trust but Pearl Dean.

Laila pulled herself up. She had reached the boulevard. Well, then, she'd run away successfully if she was all the way to the boulevard and nobody after her. She had never been alone, on foot, before, in an American city. But she was not afraid. It was time to put the house, and the people there, behind her. What was to be done next?

She meant to get to Pearl, of course, and hide her head. Laila put aside her longing for Pearl's presence to consider how to get to it. She knew the name of the woman at whose house Pearl was staying. Estelle. Estelle Fleming. But Laila did not know any street or number.

She had nothing in her hands. Her head was bare. It didn't cross her mind to find a phone book and look up the number or to use a telephone. It hadn't crossed her mind to bring some money. She was all alone and empty-handed and the great city stretched miles below and all around her. But she was not afraid. People would be kind.

She thought she would find a taxicab, as Jonas always had. And the driver would know. She would ask him to take her to Mrs. Estelle Fleming's house. So she stood on the sidewalk and her long black hair stirred and whispered on her back against the coral colour of the suit she wore as she began to peer into the traffic for a taxicab.

A man, on the sidewalk, couldn't keep his eyes off her. His wife used her elbow. "Hollywood," she said contemptuously.

Clive Breen was mortified. He could not help feeling that everyone on the bus knew slyly what had happened to his car. Of all the humiliations a man must face, to be stripped of his wheels, his mobility, especially in Los Angeles, was one of the worst Clive could imagine. For two hundred lousy bucks! He'd get it and throw it in their faces. Maybe he'd get the whole twelve hundred and throw that.

Meanwhile he didn't have two hundred or even twenty. He was overdrawn and he was angry, thinking of it. Five thousand dollars was peanuts. How could a man operate on peanuts?

Sometimes he wished he had made a little more fuss of Uncle Jonas. Clive hadn't cared for him. All Jonas's yarns had seemed to Clive to be the purest guff. Him and his pearls. Him and his Chinese connections. Clive, himself, swallowed much taller tales every week in the year with no trouble, but they were "deals" whereby he and some like-minded associates would sell something they hadn't got yet for fabulous profits. These deals were different. They were in his own idiom. Pearls he couldn't take.

But there must have been pearls or something, he thought glumly. Jonas had left half a million to an eighteen-year-old girl. He thought about his cousin Laila. Kid didn't know anything. She had, he happened to know, twenty thousand bucks in a checking account. What a ridiculous place that was for twenty grand to be!

Clive didn't think Stirling was any business man and what did Dee know? Dee had her five thousand in a savings bank and that was ridiculous, too. Why was it that people who couldn't see over the horizon were always the ones who had the capital?

He thought he could get two or three hundred from Laila all right if he ever got up there on this damn pokey bus. One-thirty already. He prided himself on having been darned nice to Laila. Clive fancied that the ladies fancied him. He was thirty. He thought of

48

himself as tall and handsome. He thought of himself as smooth and shrewd, although a little unlucky. He had not the slightest suspicion that the inside of his sleek head was filled with confused and childish stuff of which bad luck is made.

Now he was remembering bitterly that he was a married man. Nedda wasn't living with him. It had gone *pfft* long ago. He'd never felt the necessity of sinking money in a divorce. Now he wished he'd bought a divorce with some of that five thousand. If he was divorced, say, and could have played up to Laila. . . . He happened to know that if Laila got married and had a kid the kid got it *all*.

But no, he thought. Maybe he wouldn't be happy marrying for money. *Something* in what this guy Talbot had said. He couldn't have gone through with it, the necessary romantic attitude, the necessary lies. Clive felt himself honourable. He would owe, for the money, a good counterfeit of love. But, he couldn't have done it for Laila. She made him nervous. Odd little thing. And besides they were cousins and he didn't know if that would matter.

He wished his cousin Dee would mind her business. Fine thing, *her* living up there!

His mind went back to the department of ways and means. Tell Laila he needed five hundred. Why not? If Dee wasn't around to ask questions why Laila'd never know the difference. And he did have deals pending. Might as well try for a little margin.

He saw his corner coming up and he lurched down the aisle. Now he'd have to climb up about six blocks but maybe he could call a cab to get down again, if he was lucky this time.

So he pressed his foot to the sidewalk and there,

standing next to the florist's booth, looking so odd with that long black hair that you couldn't miss her, was his cousin Laila!

Chapter Six

She saw him and her face changed and she came toward him.

"Hey, Laila! For the love of Mike, what are you doing?"

"Oh, Clive!"

"Are you *alone?*" he asked incredulously.

"Clive, will you help me find a taxicab? I don't know what's the matter. They look at me but they don't stop. Clive, will you help me?"

"Sure, honey. Sure I will." He felt a touch of the exultant sensation that told him this was luck! "Where you going in a taxicab?"

"I want to go to Pearl Dean. I must."

"Anything the matter?" He had his eyes squinted; it was a muscular habit. Long ago, he had thought it made him look shrewd and inscrutable.

"I want to be with Pearl for a while," Laila said, sounding desperate. "Please, Clive."

"But listen, can't Sidney take you in the car?" She shook her head and Clive thought, What's up? He said, "Well, why shouldn't you go to see Pearl Dean if you want to? Where is she, honey?"

"At the house of Mrs. Fleming."

"What's the address?"

"A taxicab will take me."

"Honey," Clive said, "you'll have to tell him where to go."

"But I don't know," she said. He stood there marvelling, and then her face changed, "But, Clive, you do know. One time you drove Dee and me."

"Did I?"

"Of course. Clive, drive me there in your car! I'd be so grateful."

Clive agreed that she would. He said regretfully, "I just don't happen to have my car today, honey. But don't you worry. I'll see that you get there."

"It would be a great favour," Laila said warmly.

He smiled. He took her arm and pretended to peer up and down the busy boulevard. "Funny thing. You know, I was on my way to ask *you* a favour."

"Oh, were you? Oh, Dee told me. You need some money, do you not?"

Clive cleared his throat. Damn Dee, he thought.

"I wish I had brought some money," Laila said, "so that I could give it to you."

He looked down on her squint-eyed. "How were you going to pay the taxi?" he inquired.

"Oh I . . .should have brought some for myself." Laila flushed. "I forgot."

Clive wanted to hoot. He thought, of all the nutty things to do, walk off without a cent of car fare! Of all the . . . ! But something hurt and quivering in her upturned face warned him not to jeer. He said carefully, "How come you forgot? Were you upset or anything?"

"Yes, I was." An expression of pure pain stained her face and vanished. "I hope you will help me. If could be with Pearl for a day or two . . ."

"A day or two," he murmured. Then he said, lightly,

although he was eaten with curiosity. "Why not? Sure, I'll help you. I tell you, though . . . do you have any cash? I mean at the house. Or . . . I suppose you've got a cheque-book someplace. You see, you won't get very far without money."

"I see," she said flushing, looking ashamed. "I forgot. I want so much to be with Pearl. I mustn't ask her to pay for me, must I?"

Clive heard the bitter hint of pain but he couldn't place it. "Well, I don't think Pearl's got an awful lot of dough," he said gently, feeling his way. "So we had better go back to the house, don't you think? And . . ."

"Oh, no!" She pulled her arm away.

He just stood there.

"I don't want to see them."

"See who?"

"Dee . . . or Andrew. Please, Clive. Don't make me . . ."

"Sssh." He thought she might burst into tears there on the street. "Of course I'm not going to make you do any-thing. But why not, honey? What did they do?"

"I want to be away . . ."

"Away from *Dee?*" She nodded, and he said, watching her face, "Well, Dee's got no real jurisdiction and cer-tainly Talbot hasn't. If you don't want to see them I don't see why you should have to." Her face showed relief and gratitude. (Gratitude, that was the thing.) "Maybe I could get the money for you," he suggested.

"Oh, could you? Oh Clive, you are kind! There is some money, I'm sure. In my dressing-table. Where my stockings are."

"How much?" asked Clive, squinting.

"Oh, there are some hundreds and some twenties, I think."

"All right," he said, swallowing his emotion. "Now, I'll tell you just what we'll do. We'll get us a cab and we'll go up there. But the cab won't turn in and you can stay in it. D'you see, honey? While I go in and get the money. That is," he added cautiously, "if you'll back me up. I don't want to be taken for a thief or anything. I mean, that *is* all right with you?"

"It would be most kind!" said Laila. "Then the taxicab could take me to Pearl."

"Of course."

"And you won't make me see them?"

"I won't even let them see *me,* if I can help it," said Clive genially. "You leave it to me, now. Clive'll fix everything."

It was a good thing, Clive Breen reflected, that Uncle Jonas's yard was such a tangle. Ideal for his purposes. He slouched inconspicuously along the tunnel of the driveway. He had a hunch he'd better try to duck Dee entirely, because that redheaded young woman would blast the facts out of him, as well he knew. He wanted to earn Laila's gratitude and put himself in line for a nice loan, as could come about as naturally as anything in the world. But Dee wouldn't approve, of course.

He thought, she's damn bossy. He knew that he himself should find out more about what was going on, should be a good deal surer than he was that for Laila to run away to Pearl Dean was right and proper.

But Clive was going to proceed, instead, on the simple premise that he was doing the girl a favour, and asking no questions because no gentleman would.

Talbot's convertible was standing in the drive.

So Clive edged along the side of the house. Laila's big Chrysler wasn't in. He could see that. The garage was

54

wide open. Then he saw Sidney Dickett come running around from behind the garage, hurry inside, fling open the door that led to the stairs to his living-quarters above. Clive froze in the shrubbery as Sidney's feet pounded upward.

But then Clive noticed that there was no upstairs window on this side of the garage building, so he seized the chance to slip around to the back door of the big house. He saw no one in the little back entry.

From the entry he could see that there was no one in the kitchen.

From the kitchen, he touched softly the swinging pantry door. No one in the pantry, and that was all right, but from the pantry, now, suddenly, he could hear their voices in the hall. So he hesitated. He chose the third door out of the pantry, the one that led to the great dark dining-room which lay at the right side of the staircase.

He came softly around the huge hideous carved sideboard. He was in the house and near the stairs, but he could get no farther. He stood still, in there, listening.

Dee's voice, sharp and annoyed, was crying, "Hello? Hello? Mrs. Fleming? Mrs. Fleming?"

"Let me talk to her," Talbot said loudly.

"She hung up!"

"Call her back *again.*"

"She won't talk. She just keeps saying Pearl isn't there. She won't take a message. We're wasting time."

"What's the matter with the woman?"

"She must be whacky. She's one of Pearl's nearest and dearest. She probably is. We're wasting time."

"No, Dee . . ."

"Can't we just *go?*" Dee begged. "I can't stand this telephoning!"

"All right." Andy sounded tense and yet calm. "We can

try trailing her. It's possible. The pink suit and that hair."

Lorraine, the maid, piped up. "Miss Dee, what must I do?"

"Stay here, Lorraine," Dee told her. "You stay by the telephone. Dr. Stirling might call. We'll try to keep in touch, too. Don't worry too much, Lorraine. We're going to find her."

"Oh, Miss Dee, I hope so."

"Stirling is moving heaven and earth," Andy said. "The police may pick her up before we even . . ."

"Come on! Come on!" Dee cried and the door rattled.

Clive heard the rush of their feet, the slam of the door, the roar of the car. Well, they knew the kid had run away and they were after her, all right. He wondered numbly if the cab that waited just around the corner of Jonas's property was going to stand out like a sore thumb in that neighbourhood.

But then he heard Lorraine bat at the pantry door and that was his chance, of course, to sneak upstairs where the money was.

In Laila's room he crept to the dressing-table. His sensations were guilty and disagreeable. He opened the right top drawer and the sight of the bills washed his guilt away in a flood of resentment. Money lying around! Mixed in with beads and boxes, stockings and brassieres!

There was eight hundred dollars in bills. Clive rolled it neatly together and put it in his pocket. His lips were tight with anger. He looked around, a little glassy-eyed with his sense of outrage. He opened a closet. There was a long thin-wool blue coat. He took it quietly off the hanger. There was a floppy hat, made of dark red felt, a kind of tam-o'-shanter. He took it off the pretty little hat-

56

stand on the shelf. He hesitated and then he picked up a shining little black handbag.

The top of his mind was full of virtue. He would give value for value received. Promised to get Laila to Pearl Dean, and so he would. No one would stop her because she wore a coral-pink suit and her hair down. She was pretty conspicuous in that bright garment with the long black hair. Clive already had a feeling that it might be just as well if he got to Pearl's (and earned the money) and no one knew he'd had anything to do with it. He thought, if he asked her, Laila wouldn't mention him. She would be so grateful.

He crept to the top of the stairs and reconnoitred. All was still. He stared down, then pulled his foot back because he heard the voices, and he stood, poised, uneasy, and dismayed.

"Guess it was crazy to think she might be up in *our* room," Sidney was saying. "But that was one place I didn't look, so I hadda. So they went, eh?"

Lorraine was softly sobbing.

"Why don't you wait until there's something to cry about?" said Sidney in tones of rough comfort. "They'll find her, all right."

Lorraine said, "Poor Mrs. Vaughn, though. Poor Mrs. Vaughn."

"It really made her sick, eh?"

"It poisoned her, Sid. She's going to die."

"Who said? The doctor?" Sidney bristled against the thought of death.

Lorraine's sobs grew wilder.

"Just darn lucky *you* didn't get none," Sid said, roughly tender. "Listen, if Miss Laila got the same poison, how come she feels so spry she can run away?"

"Because Mrs. Vaughn ate it yesterday and Laila ate it

today . . . this morning."

"You mean it don't affect you for a while?"

"For hours, Sid. For sixteen hours, anyhow, and maybe longer."

"Sixteen hours! What d'you mean?"

"All I know is, that's what they *said*. They said if they can give her some kind of serum or something before sixteen hours go by, then she'll be perfectly all right. But if she gets sick of it, like Mrs. Vaughn did, then it's too late."

Sidney said bluntly, "Too late?"

"For the serum or whatever it is."

"D'you mean she'll *die?*" asked Sidney, awe-struck.

"She'll die," wailed his wife. "And she's too young. For her it's different. She shouldn't die, Sid, and everything in front of her . . . oh . . ."

"Listen," he said, "save it. They'll get hold of her. Where's she going to go? Sixteen hours is a lot of hours. Come on, make some coffee, why don't we?"

"I won't touch food in this house."

"Now, listen, everything ain't poisoned. Coffee ain't food. Come on, I'll fix it."

"I got to stay by the . . ."

"We can hear the phone."

At the top of the stairs a figure leaned on the wall and it was motionless. When several minutes had gone by and the silence below continued, the figure stirred. It began to come slowly down.

It put its feet close to the wall where there would be no creaking.

It flitted across to the front door.

It slipped through.

It plunged silently away.

Chapter Seven

The top of Clive's mind said crossly, I don't know what they were talking about. I couldn't half hear it, anyhow.

But under this, he was wondering if Laila was running away, like the crazy kid she was, from something that had her scared, because she didn't understand it.

The top of his mind answered, *Laila* didn't say anything about anything like that to *me*.

But deep under, he happened to know a fact or two. He didn't let the knowledge up too far into his consciousness, but the facts were there. A hot glow like a halo embalmed them. By Jonas's will, if little Laila died, childless and unmarried, then the fortune split. Share and share alike, it came to her cousins, Dee Allison and Clive Breen.

Clive was not a thief. He had come and gone quite secretly, and he had somebody else's money in his pocket. But he was not a thief, of course.

No more could he ever be a murderer. All he was doing, he was doing the kid a simple favour. He didn't really know a thing but what she'd told him, which wasn't much. And you don't want to believe everything you happen to half overhear.

He hadn't really heard, at all.

No one could ever say that he had.

What if he'd gone up to Laila's room and down

again only now, while they were drinking the coffee in the kitchen, and there had been no voices in the hall? It might just as easily have happened to work out that way.

If, deep, he was doing arithmetic, he chose not to know it.

Estelle Fleming put down the phone and stood beside it to make sure it was not going to ring again. When it did not, she patted it with satisfaction.

Somebody had told her long ago that she was a piquant type. She had a sharp little nose, a sharp little chin, and birdlike mannerisms, much abrupt shifting and tilting of the head. But her eyes weren't birdbright any more.

"Dearest Pearl," she murmured. People were so impossible, so often selfishly excited about their own affairs. Dearest Pearl would be in, soon, and would need to renew her vitality. She would lie in the light on the sun porch. It was a favourite spot. Estelle quivered to think that Pearl was fond of it.

Nothing was going to induce so understanding and true a friend as Estelle to delay or prevent the sacred process, so necessary to Pearl's well-being. "Estelle, your devotion . . ." Pearl had said so often.

Sometimes she wished Pearl would stay on with her forever. But Pearl would leave her soon; the spirit would move her on.

Ah, during the precious days of Pearl's visit, not one moment of Pearl's peace would be disturbed. Pearl would *need* her quiet hour. People never understood.

* * *

Dr. John Stirling, in his office, surrounded by his hive of busy healing, buzzed into the telephone.

"Now, then," he said, "I've told you the facts. I'm a reputable citizen. Check with the county health office. If you can go after a criminal you can certainly pass the word and pick that girl up. I'm telling you in no uncertain terms that she has got to be in this hospital by midnight tonight. And I don't care if you bring her in a Black Maria. Now, what are you going to do about it?"

"Give me the description, Doctor," the voice said without excitement.

"Five foot, two or three. Slender. Long black hair, and I mean long. To her waist. Brown eyes. Wearing a pinkish-coloured suit, no hat."

"Caucasian?"

"Yes, white."

"Age?"

"Eighteen."

"Any scars, marks?"

"No. Now listen. She's somewhere loose in this city. And she's been poisoned and she doesn't know it. Now, how soon do you think . . . ?"

"We can try," the voice said noncommittally.

"You sound like you hear a thing like this six days a week," snapped the doctor.

"Well, no. We don't," the voice said with traces of amusement.

"Get on it, will you?"

"We'll get on it."

The doctor hung up and said to his secretary, "Get me a radio station. A big network. Get me all of them, Mary."

Dee and Andy flew out of the house. Andy piled in behind the wheel. He turned the key and the motor rumbled. Dee slammed the door.

"Where?"

"Downhill. There's nothing the other way."

The tyres clawed the gravel. The blue convertible snaked around the narrow drive and wrenched to the right.

Dee clenched her naked hands and bent her whole mind to this hunting.

These streets wound between expensive houses with extensive grounds. There would be no pedestrians. "Cab!" cried Dee. "What is it doing parked? No fare. I can't see anyone."

Andy braked and backed the car. Dee would have flown out but he leaned across her and barred her in with his arm. "How long you been standing there?" he shouted at the cab-driver.

The cabby adjusted his hat. "About a minute," he howled back. "Why?"

"You see anybody walking by?"

"Nope. Whatsamatter?"

"Waiting on a fare? Man or woman?"

"Waiting on a man. Whatsa idea, bud?"

Andy trod on the gas and the wheels spun. "Can't stop and tell the whole story every time we ask a question. Not if we want to hurry."

"That's so," agreed Dee. Peering hard at the walls and the hedges as they tore by, she thought that every gate, every door, was at least a possible place for Laila to have slipped through. The magnitude of the search now appalled her. "How do we know we aren't passing her by?"

"We don't know," Andy said grimly. "But you have to start on probability. You're wondering whether she went into one of these strange houses? The chances are she wouldn't."

"You mean it might be easier than it looks?"

"It's not easy. The possibilities are in the millions. Police department has a better chance when it comes to a search."

"We can't search," Dee said, "we must track her."

"Laila's most probably on her way to Pearl Dean. We know that."

"Yes, I suppose we do know that." Dee began to will herself to look at the world with Laila's eyes.

"Got to try using our heads, Dee, the best we can." He was cold with resolve.

"But we aren't sure where Pearl Dean was going. And Laila just might know her plans."

"The first thing Laila would do, most probably, is to skip right on down to the boulevard. That's where there's transportation, Dee. Now if we could discover, for instance, that she took a bus . . ."

"I don't think," said Dee slowly, "that Laila would take a bus."

"We can find out."

"Remembering how little she understands," said Dee. "What's worrying me — she might fall in with anybody. Anybody might pick her up . . ."

"Don't worry. Think."

Dee imagined herself to be Laila. "Yes, she would go down to the boulevard."

"Somebody will have seen her." Andy was looking straight ahead. "If I'd any idea . . . If I'd kept my big mouth . . ."

"Let's not 'if' it up," Dee said. Her own heart was

heavy with the weight of 'if'. She felt the cold air where her ring had been, the cold breeze blowing. If she had listened up on the hill with any real sympathy. If she had said, "Andy, I understand. I respect what you are trying to do. I will help if I can. I will hurry to break away from this task. I will not be so proud." But she must not look back. She must try to imagine herself to be Laila, with Laila's limitations.

"I think she'd take a cab," said Dee. "I'm almost sure that's what she'd do."

Up on the hill, behind them, Laila got up off the cab floor. "Thank you," she said softly.

"What's it about?" asked the cab-driver. His eyes were lively with curiosity. "I guess you don't want to tell me, huh?"

She laced her fingers in and out. "I didn't want them to see me," she said faintly. "So thank you very much."

"Don't thank me. I didn't tell no lies, Miss." The driver was a chunky little man with a nut-brown face. His name was Vince Procter. Now he began to fiddle with his intercom. "Waiting on a fare," he said into it and gave his number. "Seventy-three. Meter's going."

"O.K. Seventy-three," said the spectral voice. Vince saw in his mirror the eyes on this kid with the weird hair-do as they bugged out. This amused him. He was curious, but from his experience, he figured this was boy-and-girl stuff, probably. He liked a plot, but he didn't go for romances. He liked a mystery. He yawned.

Clive Breen came sliding around the shrubs on the corner.

"O.K., driver. Make it the drugstore, corner of Almond and Western."

The driver saluted.

"Laila," Clive said in her ear nervously, "are you all right?"

"I'm fine."

"Look," Clive leaned and said to the driver, "did you know you can take the next right and come out on Vermont? Less traffic that way."

The cab-driver didn't mind traffic, nor did he even agree, but he didn't mind obliging. So he swung right and Clive sighed and settled back. He had Laila's handbag and now he put five twenties in it. As he gave it to her, his sensations were those of generosity and thoughtfulness. He said in a low voice, "Now you're all set, honey."

"Oh, Clive," she said gratefully, "you did get it! You are kind! Is that my coat?"

He nodded. "Let's not . . . uh . . . talk too loud. Slide into it, honey. Could you stuff all that hair up under this thing? I thought maybe . . ."

She wiggled into the coat that concealed her coral suit. She began to wind her hair into a great cable. She leaned and whispered, "They are looking for me, are they not? I saw them, Clive."

He nodded and watched her face. "Yeah, I think they're looking for you."

"Oh, are they worried?" asked Laila. "I didn't think. I *never* think." She looked as if she were going to cry.

He shrugged. "If you didn't tell them where you were off to, I guess they'd worry." He watched her.

"Oh, Clive, after I get to Pearl, then you can tell them where I am? Then they wouldn't worry any more?"

His face changed, somehow. He said, soothingly, "Why sure, honey. Whatever you say. That's what I'm here for."

Now that her hair was wound up under the dark-red tam, her small face looked quite different, as did the shape of her head with her neck bare.

Andy and Dee were taking too long in the florist's shop. The florist had seen Laila. He recognized the description immediately, as they could tell. But he wanted to get the straight of it before he would answer any questions. He was a cautious man. He had a weather-beaten suspicious face and it would not open.

"She's my cousin," pleaded Dee, "and she has to be taken to hospital quickly. Oh please, if you can tell us anything . . ."

She could see he didn't believe the girl he'd seen was ill. Dee realized that Andy was right. It took forever to explain. Laila didn't look ill. And the approach was wrong. Even her urgency was having a bad effect. It would have been better to seem casual, easier to get the answers if the answers didn't seem to matter so much. So she walked away and controlled herself to stand quietly behind the flowers on the glass shelves across the window.

There were a man and a woman in the shop, puttering over the displays, the woman cooing. But the man was listening, and Dee began to watch him out of the corner of her eye.

Andy said in a reasonable tone, "We are trying to find out whether she took a bus or a cab or what. And which direction she went. If you happened to notice, it would certainly help a lot." Andy leaned on the

66

counter and seemed relaxed.

"I didn't notice," said the florist with an air of relief.

"But you saw her? She got this far?"

"Saw her, I guess," the florist said grudgingly. "I don't think I can help you."

Andy glanced sceptically around at all the glass.

"Listen," the florist said. "All right. There was a girl with that kind of hair. So how do I know it's the one you mean? All I can say, she stood out there for a while. Then she went outa my sight. Could have seen a bus pulling in. I didn't notice." He made as if to go about his business.

"You didn't see a cab pull over?"

"All I know, it kinda looked like she saw something." The man was warming up a little. "Started to walk quick. But I didn't see where she went."

By now, Dee was sure that the male customer had something on his mind. She walked quickly toward him. "You saw her, didn't you, sir?" The man gaped like a goldfish.

But the woman, a tightly corseted, highly perfumed, slightly hennaed matron, took his arm suddenly, "My husband and I didn't see anyone, Miss," she said coldly, to this slim and spectacularly pretty girl in soft green, whose glorious hair had never been touched up at all.

The man began to speak unreadable volumes with his eyes. "We're in a hurry," the woman said. "Come, Charles. Never mind the flowers." And the man wrenched his eyes away from Dee's blue stare.

Andy swung around.

"They saw her," said Dee. "They know something."

Outside the couple were hurrying toward their car.

"I'd just like to know what it's all about," the man

67

complained. "I'm not going to . . ."

"Not going to get mixed up," said the woman viciously. "And spoil our trip. That type," she added. "Hollywood."

Dee was running after them and Andy behind her. The woman got into the driver's seat. She had the car started and in motion so fast that the man was forced to close the door in Dee's very face.

He bawled out of the window, "She spoke to a man—" and then he was gone.

Dee would have started to run again but Andy held her.

"Wait."

She was straining to see after that car, to see which way it would go; it was in her mind to chase, to insist.

Andy held her. "You can't catch them. Get calm, Dee."

Dee had soft-soled fabric slippers on her bare feet and when she stamped her foot the pavement stung.

"*She* thinks he just wants to talk to a pretty girl," she said. "But maybe—"

"Use your head. We can't go chasing off on tangents."

"Laila spoke to a man! He could describe the kind of man—"

"What good would that do? Maybe she spoke to a man." Andy was crisp and tense. "Maybe not. This guy had a roving eye, all right. Wanted to get in on the excitement."

"He wanted to get in on the—fun?" said Dee bitterly. "All right. We'll discount it. What are we going to do to find her?"

"Just stop boiling over," he said, a little coolly. "*I'm* going to ask in the real estate office."

Dee, stumbling behind him, looked at the traffic, moving, flowing, and saw the whole city fluid, everything shifting, people who crossed Laila's path now moving elsewhere. She saw how this pursuit could be a crazy zig-zag, how they could be blown this way and that like a piece of paper being buffeted by conflicting breezes. Unless they were cool and careful. She thought of Laila, who wouldn't be cool and careful at all, who would not know danger from kindness.

The bland faces in the real estate office were turning politely.

Chapter Eight

Vince Procter made change for a twenty. His fares turned into the drugstore and he pulled away. He spoke into his intercom. The spectral voice repeated, "Seventy-three." It lost its impersonal character suddenly. "Say, Vince. Just told to get word out. Keep your eyes open for a girl, about five foot three, with long black hair, wearing a pink suit. They want to get her to a hospital."

"What's the matter with her?" Vince was nothing at all but astonished.

"She's got to get some kind of treatment. Some doctor is calling the cab companies. It's O.K. We checked with the police."

"Is that right?" Vince drawled. His eyes flickered. "What's the story?"

"They want her at the Greenleaf Hospital before midnight. That's all I know."

"Before midnight, eh? Is there a reward or something?"

"Didn't say."

"Lemme know if you hear that."

"Roger." The voice got impersonal. "Where are you?"

Vince told. "In action," he snapped. "Code red." This meant that he had a fare and would leave the intercom open.

He didn't have a fare . . . yet. But cab number seventy-three waltzed around in a U turn. Vince Procter was pleased and excited. Boy-and-girl stuff might bore him but intrigue he loved. He had always wanted to be a spy.

Clive closed the phone book. "O.K., honey, now we've got the number, we can go. Say, what if Pearl isn't there?" (He knew she wasn't there yet, but he avoided remembering how it was that he knew.)

"But she was going there, Clive," said Laila with a lost look on her face.

"Probably Dee's going to guess where you are, honey. You might run into Dee."

Laila said, restlessly, "Could we go there, Clive? You do know where to go?"

"We'll go," said Clive kindly. "I guess we can cross that bridge when we come to it." He looked at his watch. It was two o'clock.

Outside, he made an imperious gesture and a cab slid in. Clive began to give the Fleming address but he changed his mind in mid-air. "You know Inglewood? You know Fernwald? Make it the eighteen hundred block on Fernwald, east side of the street. I'll tell you when we get there."

The driver saluted and Clive got in beside Laila. "I just remembered there's an alley," he told her. "Maybe we can kinda sneak in the back way. Lay low and see if Dee is there. This is hide-and-seek, eh? Ever play that, where you lived when you were little?"

Laila put her head back. "When I was very little," she said. She was thinking that she was older. Her face was sad.

Clive had a nervous appreciation of her mood. He put himself in the pattern of her older cousin, wise and fond.

"Aw now, honey, tell Clive? Why don't you? I know something must have happened. What's got you so upset?"

Laila felt he was kind. "Andrew explained to me," she said bravely, "I'm taking too much from Dee and I am a trouble to both of them."

"That Talbot," Clive snorted. "You don't want to worry your head about anything *he* says. As a matter of fact, Dee takes too much on herself, if you ask me. She's bossy, you know. She's even kept me from trying to . . . uh . . . be a better friend to you. She really has. She wants to do it all."

"She's been too kind," said Laila forlornly. "I don't know, Clive. Mamma was always kind. Jonas was kind. I thought it was easy."

"There, now . . ."

"But I think it is easy for Pearl to be kind, don't you, Clive?"

"Sure it is, honey. Why wouldn't it be? It's only Dee and that Talbot who make such a thing of it. I hope they don't get Dr. Stirling all stirred up, though. I . . ."

"I don't think," she whispered, "Dr. Stirling is so kind."

"Well, he's a bossy type, too," said Clive complacently. "And those medics get that way. Always saying the word between life and death . . ."

"I know," she whispered.

The cab's intercom was buzzing. "Seventy-three," said the driver irritably. "Long haul to Inglewood."

"Pickup on Western." The voice gave an address.

"Take me an hour, hour and a half . . ."

"Skip it," the voice said.

Clive was gazing numbly at the back of the driver's head. He felt a freezing wonder. This wasn't another cab. This was the same one! He had been thinking, that with her coat . . .

Well, he hadn't done anything wrong. What did he have to worry about? Laila was emotionally upset. That's all he knew. As a matter of fact, he realized, that was all he dared to know. He'd already made his decision to be ignorant. He'd go ahead, turn the kid over to Pearl Dean. He began to think over what little he knew about this Pearl Dean.

"Pearl used to know your mother, didn't she?" he murmured.

"Pearl knows her well," said Laila.

Startled by the present tense, Clive sucked his tooth. Who was this Pearl Dean and what was her angle? Spirit stuff? Did she like Laila or Laila's money or what, he wondered?

At two p.m. the blue convertible was sliding south. Dee and Andy had found out no more on that corner. Now they were doing the most sensible thing they could think to do. They were going to the Fleming house in the hope that Laila was also going there.

Dee could feel, piling up behind them, the vast network of streets they had not searched and could not search for one small girl. She saw, sliding by, all the variety of places—cleaners, drugstore, appliance shop, cocktail bar, parking lot, movie theatre, shoe repair, linen store, luggage, laundry and hamburger stand. And the apartments and courts, motels, and houses, houses, houses. She observed the traffic, buses and trolleys, the trucks and the taxis, and the cars, cars, cars. Laila was a needle in a haystack, just as hard to find as that.

She was beginning to surmise that it was a very peculiar kind of haystack. The couple at the florist's, for instance. If he had not been a man with an eye for a pretty figure, if his wife had not long known and resented this—if another kind of couple had seen Laila there—she and Andy might know more than they now knew. All the "ifs" were people—thoughts in people's heads.

If Laila had spoken to ask direction of some solid citizen, it was one thing. If she'd spoken to some rackety, pimply youth, it was another. If she'd spoken to someone who could not sense Laila's own innocent difference—haystack? It was a labyrinth. There were dark twists in it.

Andy glanced at her face. "Tell me," he said, "what would Laila do if she gets to the Fleming house and Pearl Dean is not there?"

"I don't know. Everything depends on so many other things. When, where, and what kind of person—on this Mrs. Fleming, maybe. You can't—" She wanted to express her feeling, her vision—but he interrupted.

"I think we've got to call Stirling back. We've been out of touch too long."

"You think he may have heard something?"

"I think he may. Anyhow, I'd like to suggest the idea of a cab to him. I have a hunch she'll never get as far as Inglewood. It's the hell-and-gone south . . ."

"Suggest a cab to the police, you mean?"

"Yes, and let Stirling handle all that. He's stationary. Better position than we are to find her, actually."

"Andy, if she talked to a man—don't you see it makes such a difference what kind—"

"This is geography, Dee. It's places. She's somewhere. *We* can't turn every stone. But the police can do

74

that."

She shook her head, "You have to follow something. We have a chance to find her if we—"

"I don't care who finds her," he said in sudden anguish. "I just doubt we're doing much good—roaring around. I think we've got to call, and I need gas."

So he pitched the wheel over and the car dashed into a gas station on a corner, one that shrilled to the eye a block away, all gaily decked with coloured banners. Pitched them into a nightmare.

Horns blew. Bells rang. People seemed to spring from the ground. Flash bulbs went off in their faces. A grinning man in white overalls grasped Andy's hand and pumped it violently.

Somebody cried, "Hey, Red! Hey, look this way, Red!"

Somebody said, "Get the girl with Joe, you guys. She's photogenic and how!"

"It gives me great pleasure . . ." the man in white was booming into a microphone that had jumped up from some place, "to present you, sir with this fifty dollar savings bond . . ."

"Wait a minute, Joe, will ya?" screamed somebody. "Wait a minute . . ."

"Wassa matter!"

"The mike's dead."

Somebody cried, "Why ain't I loaded with colour!"

"Listen," the white-clad man said confidentially, his breath tinged with alcohol, "this is just a little stunt, see. You hit the jackpot folks. You are our one-millionth customer. Whatd'ya know, eh? Surprised?"

Stunned, Dee could feel Andy gathering control of himself. "How long will this take?" he asked in measured calm.

"Five minutes. Ten. Aw, you're in no hurry. There's prizes. Fifty dollar bond for the gent and nylons for the lady."

"O.K., Joe. On the mike, now."

"Folks. . ." boomed Joe.

Andy said under his breath to Dee, "I think we'll get out faster if we sit quiet."

People were collecting, lured by the knot already about them, by the noise. The pavement was vanishing. Dee's jaw trembled. "I suppose you're right."

"I'd like to hit him and jump, but there's a cop. A wrangle could take us even longer . . ."

"I suppose you're right."

She looked at his face. It was bleak. Dee said, "You couldn't know . . .

"Dammit," he said, "if I'd *known —* " His jaw worked.

"Andy, shall I get out? Go on alone?"

You'll never get away," he said bitterly, "you're too good-looking."

It hurt. She put her bare hand to her mouth.

"Aw, give us a smile, Red, why don'tcha?" somebody was pleading. "And say, listen, you'll sign a release, won'tcha? So you'll be in a big old ad. What can it hurt you?"

They were all grinning like monkeys, entranced with their stunt and their fun. Dee thought, It's the same thing. They're all thinking their own thoughts, each following his own line of attention. All the lines crisscross and intersect, and here they happen to hold us.

"Smile," said Andy savagely.

She smiled as best she could.

Under direction, Vince Procter pulled up at an alley's mouth. Making change, he glanced slyly down the alley. Pulling away, he saw in his quickly angled mirror that the man and the girl who wore a pink suit under that blue coat just stood there on the sidewalk. Waiting for him to get away. Uh huh. But Vince wasn't going away. He was playing spy.

He scooted. But he braked suddenly. Parked. Went at a fast walk back. Head around a brick corner, he saw them in the alley. They went straight in, between backyards. He made a note and a careful count, when they turned and went left, about a third of the way along.

He went scrambling back to his cab and spoke to the office. "Say, any more on that girl?"

"No more."

"Been found yet?"

"Haven't heard."

"And no reward or anything like that, eh?"

"Listen, Vince," said the voice, "we're swamped, see. Get back and make that pickup. Skip the buried treasure. Will ya? Don't go cruising around looking to be a hero. Because if you do . . ."

"You'll mention it upstairs," said Vince. "Yeah."

"You know," the voice warned. "You know the time you thought you saw a murderer. You know the time . . ."

"O.K., O.K. Code black." He cut the communication.

And what you don't know ain't going to hurt you, either, he thought truculently. Hell with that pickup. It was a little after three p.m. He had ideas. He'd listened with pricked-up ears to every word he could catch between his late passengers. He hadn't heard anything about illness or treatment. Could be it wasn't the right girl. Could be it was, too. If so, there was a plot going on. Vince loved plots. And he knew where they had gone.

Mrs. Flemming's house was a neat stucco, bright, new, and painted blue. It was very much like a million others, along a thousand new streets that spread incredibly over the basic desert of this vast and sparkling plain between the mountains and the sea. An alley skirted her backyard and the single garage that stood on a back corner of her lot. Here, on the rather shabby lawn, Pearl Dean's aluminium house trailer was peacefully standing. Beside it was Pearl's coupé.

"Oh, Pearl!" Laila began to run up the flagstone path.

Clive saw the door open in the glassed porch. He saw Laila hurl herself upon the massive figure in the black crêpe dress. He settled, mentally, for the seven hundred dollars in his pocket. He advanced tentatively, his thoughts wiggling and squirming, twining and scrambling. Suppose Dee was here? Then he had better be ready with innocence and shock. But, if Dee was not here . . .

He began to think she was not. For Laila was talking, pleading, and Pearl Dean, for all her massive air of serenity, was surprised. He began to wonder once more about this Pearl. How would she react? She didn't, he remembered, think much of modern medicine. She feuded with Stirling. He advanced, thoughts tangling in his head.

Pearl Dean was crooning over the girl, who simply clung to her. At the same time, the big woman's huge eyes checked off Clive's advancing figure and her ears heeded the approach of her hostess within the house.

Pearl said softly, "Estelle?"

"Yes, dearest Pearl?" The sharp little old face was

stiff with resentment of this invasion, with jealousy.

"I am so happy that this has happened *here*," said Pearl very softly. "Only in your house can I be so certain of a generous and understanding heart. May I bring this child inside, Estelle, and shall we see if we can help her?"

"Dearest Pearl! How can you ask!" cried Mrs. Fleming.

"Come, Laila. Come, lamb . . . Yes, Mr. Breen?"

Clive said, "How do you do? She was so anxious to find you, Miss Dean. I . . . don't exactly know what this is all about."

"Clive has been most kind," said Laila. "Pearl, may I stay? Please keep me?"

"Of course, darling. Now, go to Estelle, little darling. Estelle has the kindest of hearts. You shall find nothing but love and kindness in this place."

"Ah, poor darling," said Estelle, hypnotized by praise.

"What is it?" asked Pearl Dean, moving rather quickly to Clive.

"Talbot must have said some sharp things to her," Clive said hesitantly. "That's about what I can make out. Told her she's a lot of trouble for Dee. Hurt her feelings."

"Ah" said Pearl, her nostrils vibrating.

"Anyhow, she acts heartbroken, says she doesn't want to see them for a while."

"See Andrew Talbot?"

"Or Dee."

"Or Dee!"

"Poor kid's pretty upset," said Clive nervously. "I happened to bump into her and I didn't know what else I should do. Has Dee called here?"

Pearl said, "No."

"She will," Clive said. All the while Pearl's great eyes examined him and he squinted at her. "They'll be hunting for Laila—Dee and Talbot."

"Every heart has a right to heal alone," said Pearl.

"They don't know where she's gone, you see. They'll be worried."

"They should be worried," said Pearl sternly. "Worried and ashamed."

"I guess I've got to let them know. Otherwise . . ."

"Yes?"

"If they tell Dr. Stirling she's missing, he's going to have the cops out after her."

Pearl Dean began to breathe heavily. She looked behind her where Laila was sitting on a rattan couch, sipping a glass of water. Estelle Fleming had removed the ugly tam and the black hair had tumbled down.

Pearl said, "I thought better of Dee. I warned her. I warned her that Laila could be hurt. It is guilt, Mr. Breen."

"What do you mean?" Clive looked startled.

"Talbot's guilt. Talbot's temptation, which he resents. He takes his own guilt out on that lovely child."

"Lousy break for the poor kid," muttered Clive.

Pearl turned and took strides. "Laila," she boomed, "would you like to go with Pearl to the sea?"

"Oh, Pearl, please! Oh, Pearl, could we?" The small face brightened.

"Estelle," said Pearl to the stiffening body, "will you protect me?" Estelle's head cocked. "We shall go for a day," boomed Pearl. "One day. We shall watch the sun rise and the sun cross and the sun go down. And one cycle later, I'll bring her back to the city and I will myself return to you Estelle, if you will have me."

80

"Dearest Pearl! You are always welcome here! This is your home!" Estelle was all beam and pleasure, now.

So Pearl smiled in benediction and swung around to Clive, who was looking very nervous. "I know what you are thinking." Pearl bent her brow upon him. "You are thinking of the law and Dr. Stirling. The law says he is her guardian. But he guards her from nothing! The little heart must steady. She must have peace."

"Well, I . . . uh . . . think so, too," said Clive weakly.

"Heaven will not grudge us one day," cried Pearl. "Nor shall *they!* Estelle . . ."

"Dearest?"

"*You* will not say to anyone whether I came or went or with whom. I know I can trust you."

"Always — always." The birdlike little woman was pleased.

"Can I trust *you?*" Pearl inquired of Clive.

"To . . . to do wh — what?" he stammered.

"To tell Stirling she is safe with me, but not *where.*"

"Look, I . . . I sympathize. I think probably you can help her a lot, but . . ." He was jittering. "Why couldn't you call up and leave a message at the house and leave me out of it entirely."

The heavy face despised him.

"I was going to ask Laila not to say I had anything to do . . . Dee'll blow her top. She'd get it all out of me and I know it."

"Are you afraid?" said Pearl Dean. "There is nothing to fear."

He began to look less afraid. "Dee'll have a fit," he insisted, "and listen, Laila's a minor, I suppose. You know what the law might say."

"I have no fear," said Pearl sternly. "I don't take her against her will. I don't take her for long. I, myself,

81

limit the time. Even Dr. Stirling will have to take my word. And Dee would not, believe me, start that kind of public trouble."

"No," he admitted.

"I have the courage to do," said Pearl sonorously, "what I know is best for her at whatever risk to myself."

"Well, that's up to you. I'd trust you. But, I'd rather . . . I don't even want to *know* where you're going."

"You'll *not* know," said Pearl in her measured boom. "Only that we go to the sea. And we shall go, and quickly." The big woman ruminated. "I shall ask Estelle," she pronounced, "to telephone the house when we are well away."

"Of course, Pearl," chirped Mrs. Fleming. "I'll do exactly as you say. Can I help you get your things together?"

"My *dear!*" said Pearl.

"You won't need much, Pearl, if you are coming back."

"Not much at all," said Pearl comfortingly.

She stood with her fat heels heavy and she rolled her eyes. All things were arranged to her satisfaction. Now she could see that her highest duty coincided with her desire. Estelle was placated. Clive did not really count. The lovely child's face was lifted to her. A malleable child. Pearl was fond of malleable people. They fed her. They nourished something. And she loved *this* child, the sweet, teachable child. She had long yearned to have her—both for the child's dear presence and the link she was to the remembered warmth and strength of the man, Jonas Breen. She touched Laila's hair.

"Lie back, little darling," she soothed. "Do as Pearl has taught you. I won't be long."

Laila lay back.

"Mr. Breen!"

"Yes, Miss Dean?"

"Do you understand how a trailer hitch operates?"

"I think so."

"Would you please . . . ?"

"G — glad to," said Clive. He stood on a brink. His nerves were dancing. Nobody here knew anything about poison! If that Lorraine had got the facts straight and if Laila were lost for one more whole day . . . !

He turned mechanically to oblige. He opened the glass door. Laila was lying back, her face composed. Pearl leaned over and touched something on the table. "There," she said. "Breathe, darling. Renew yourself. Fix your inner eye on beauty."

Clive stumbled out into the yard.

In the sun porch, near Laila's ear, soft music began.

Chapter Nine

Dee was saying, earnestly: "We are so sorry, but, you see, we were in the most awful rush when we . . ."

Joe's face got a hurt look. "No need to be stiff about it, lady," he interrupted. "Neighbourly. Only neighbourly."

"It's not that we don't appreciate . . ." she clasped her hands. She turned her beauty on, full steam. The man must understand. She was hoping he was the kind of man who would see and believe and concede that she had a line of attention of her own.

"I don't suppose you *need* any nylons, hey?" the man muttered resentfully. "You got dozens, hey? Not like some ladies."

Dee's breath sighed in. Well, this was a *kind* of person. There *were* persons to whom physical beauty was an affront, a piece of gorgeous luck that they resented. She had guessed wrong.

"How about that gas?" said Andy pleasantly.

"Look, I'm going to put gas in. You came in for some gas. You'll get gas."

"We'll come back a million times," said Dee, smiling desperately, "if you'll just let us go, now."

"You'll get gas, neighbours," the man muttered. "I'll tell Ray to give it to ya. Check your oil, neighbour?"

"Don't bother . . ." Andy glanced at Dee.

"Joe's service, you know." The man glowered.

"O.K." Andy nodded. He said in muted reproach,

"We'll never get out of here, now he's got his feelings hurt. Only been fifteen minutes, that's really all, Dee. So be quiet?"

She twisted away. "Let him take his time," she said forlornly. "Sorry."

Clive found the keys in the little coupé and he backed it into position. He dropped the hitch mechanism over the knob on the back of the car. There was also a chain. He knew what it was for, so he unwound it and slipped the hook at the end of it over the bumper. Now Pearl's aluminium house was on her back, you might say. They might go anywhere.

He thought, with a sudden sickness of the nerves, No, no. I'd better see that they call the house right away. Then he thought, I can't do that. Because I don't know any *reason*. The resolution to wipe away for ever even his own knowledge that he had overheard anything hardened in his mind. Estelle would call the house, anyhow, a little later.

He thought, The sea? My God, there's a whole coast line!

He thought, Will Pearl tell Estelle just where they're going? He thought not. Anyhow, this Estelle was such a daffy character.

He thought, But the cops will pick up Pearl, if Stirling's got the cops . . . There's no use kidding my . . .

He thought, But how soon?

Finally, he thought, Who knows how it will work out? It's out of my hands.

He shrugged and turned away and something was thinking, . . . "even after taxes" . . .

He found he had walked back to the house and he

opened the glass door once more. It would be only decent to say Good-bye (and say once more in Laila's ear, "Don't mention me"). Peering in, he stiffened. Laila was sitting upright, pawing at the little white radio beside the couch. She said, "Oh, Clive!"

Clive hurried across. "You want it off?" All he heard was a part of a sentence ". . . asked to look out for this girl and call Madison 7911 or . . ." The voice died.

He could hear Pearl's voice booming softly somewhere else in the house. He said, numbly, "What's the matter?"

Laila threw her arms out. Her eyes were so nakedly young and transparent that he squinted, as if against a painful light. "I am not ill, Clive! I am not! I am perfectly well!"

He said automatically, "ssh . . ." He moistened his mouth. "What do you mean, ill, honey? You look O.K."

"You can see that, can't you, Clive? Why do they tell people to look out for me? I don't want to be watched for. I don't want to go to hospital."

"What's that?" he mumbled. "What about a hospital?"

"Oh, Clive, call Pearl."

"Wait a minute," he said. "I don't get this." He sat down beside her and took her hand and caressed it nervously. "Tell Clive."

"I won't go to Dr. Stirling's hospital," she said with pink spots in her cheeks. "I don't want to go there. Because Jonas . . ." She bent over. Her black hair fell around her cheeks.

"Sssh . . . tell Clive, now, honey . . ."

"I told you already."

"No, you didn't, honey." Clive was honestly bewildered.

"When I saw what Dr. Stirling did, when Jonas died."

86

"What did he do?' Clive was startled almost out of his wits. "Wait a minute. You said they were *killing* Jonas. What made you think that?"

"They were! With a—thing . . . a needle in a glass . . ."

"Hypodermic." There was a sudden trace of satisfaction in Clive's voice. Now he knew what he had not known before. Here was the secret and silly reason for Laila's dislike of Dr. Stirling. She had seen the doctor try some last measure to keep the heart going, and she didn't *know* anything. She had not understood.

"Will I be locked up?" wept Laila. "I don't care if I am."

"Oh gosh," he groaned, "honey, I'm sorry. I should have listened to you that day. I was so upset myself. I— tell me, *now.* Where were you? What did you see?"

"I was there, in the room. They didn't see me. The nurse looked at the doctor and he . . . Clive what did it mean?"

Clive drew in his chin. "I don't know," he said stiffly. His thoughts scrambled busily, whirling and wavering. "A needle, you say?"

Laila said, wildly, "What can he want me at the hospital for? I'm not ill. You know that I'm not. Why is that said on the radio?"

"What was on the radio, honey?"

"A man said people must look for me and send me to the hospital."

"You!" he said. "Are you sure?"

She nodded.

"And you don't feel sick or anything?"

"No. No. No."

He said, "Well, I can't understand it, Laila. Maybe you didn't hear . . ."

Laila was not the adept at half-hearing that he was. She said, "I did hear it. I heard my name."

His face got brick red. "We'd better call up the hospital and see what this is," he began thickly.

"No, please." She had her hands clasped as if she were praying and he looked at her. "Don't tell them where I am yet. Ask Pearl, first, what we must do."

He said, looking stupid, "You're not thinking it's a trick?"

She didn't answer.

"Dirty trick," Clive said violently, "if they're just trying to find you. You really do feel all right?"

"Yes. Yes."

"You don't look ill," he muttered. He chewed on his mouth.

"Pearl will know. If Pearl thinks it's a trick or some bad thing, then Pearl will help me."

"You mean Pearl might . . . take you to the sea, *anyway?*"

"Won't she?" said Laila.

He got up and stood rubbing his head. He could feel a deep quaking in his body. "Pearl doesn't put much faith in Stirling," he murmured.

"She thinks doctors are narrow and blind. She says they use knives when they ought not to, Clive. And lots of their pills and medicines are just superstitions."

"Do *you* think that?" said Clive.

Laila threw back her head. Her eyes were perfectly innocent. "Jonas died," she said.

Clive dropped back beside her and put his head in his hands. It wouldn't be hard to sway her. Not hard at all.

"You are upset, Clive, I can tell," she said kindly. Laila rose in her fluid grace. "But Pearl will know."

Suddenly Clive could not bear to let her run and tell.

"Pearl must take you to the hospital," he said flatly.

Laila turned, light as air. "I don't understand, Clive."

"Honey, you *can't* ask Pearl to hide you from the police."

"I . . . I wasn't . . . What do you mean?"

"If she finds out about that broadcast and she *doesn't* take you back, why she may be letting herself in for trouble."

Laila's face was flushing. "I wasn't thinking," she said in a low voice. She sat down. "I understand. I never think. Pearl will want to take me to the sea, where I want so much to go. But I must not let her, must I? I must not be trouble. I must learn that."

Clive shifted and cleared his throat.

"I would have put it all on Pearl," Laila said in a sad voice. "Will I always be a nuisance, Clive? Will I ever begin to think? For myself?"

"Some day you'll kinda have to . . ." Clive muttered.

"That's what Andrew said."

Clive gnawed his mouth. "If Pearl didn't know," he murmured, "nobody could blame her if she hadn't heard . . ."

"If we don't tell her at all!" Laila raised her clasped hands. "Then she will take me as she plans."

"Well," he said, "it looks to me like that's the only way to make it your own decision."

Her head tilted proudly. Then she turned on him that naked gaze. "But won't *you* be in trouble, then?" asked Laila with searing kindness.

He writhed. "Oh I . . . I could just be out of it. You could keep me out of it, that's all. It won't work, though, honey. I just happened to think . . . Pearl's got a radio in her car."

"I know," Laila's eyes implored him. "I don't understand radios, do you, Clive?"

He couldn't look at her.

"Clive, must I decide to go back? When I don't want to?"

He heard himself muttering craftily: "You actually saw Stirling use a hypodermic the day Jonas died?"

Laila gave him one tearful look, put her hands over her face and began to cry. "I wish I was home again. Wish I was home. I'm afraid. I'm afraid. I'm afraid. I don't understand it. I am not ill at all. I only want to go with Pearl to the sea, and be quiet. Oh, I wish I could go into the sea and cross the sea and be home and never come back and never come back. . . ."

He stared at her black head. He felt pity.

"Clive, you've been so good and kind. Is there no way?"

He said, with a sudden release, as if he saw in some crooked corner of his soul the way to be kindest of all: "Maybe I could. If I could fix that radio in her car so it won't play . . ."

"Oh, please!" cried Laila.

He said, "I will if you say so. But honey, you've got to promise me . . . if you *should* start feeling bad . . ."

"How could that be?" she cried impatiently.

He knew how it could be. He sat there with that quaking going on inside of him. It was madness to be kind to Laila, now.

Laila said, "Andrew was right. I must look after myself. But I don't know how to . . . to fix a radio. Clive, if you will do that much for me, truly, I'll never tell." She looked earnestly into his face. "You do trust me?"

Squinting against the light in her eyes that he could not meet, Clive said solemnly. "Of course I do."

Chapter Ten

When Pearl Dean, carrying her black suitcase, crossed the yard with Estelle fluttering after, Clive stepped to take the suitcase. "Miss Dean, Laila wants to ride in the trailer. It might not be a bad idea."

The bare dome of Pearl's forehead creased faintly. "It's not a comfortable way to travel, pet."

"Oh, Pearl, please!" Laila was standing in the trailer's door. "It's so darling inside, a baby house. Shall I put the suitcase under the cupboard?" She vanished.

Clive said hoarsely, "It won't make much difference. Even if she is hidden, the cops will pick *you* up as soon as they're told she's with you."

The big woman turned. "You mentioned this before. Why do you say 'cops'?"

"Don't you realize? Dee, and especially Dr. Stirling, will try everything to find her."

"Not when they know she is with *me*," said Pearl regally.

"You don't think so?" said Clive.

"What have they said about me?" Pearl was instantly suspicious.

Clive squirmed. "I hate to say this. It could be that Dr. Stirling won't think you're very good for Laila."

The woman swelled with a vision of future anger. "If they do *that*," she said, containing her anger, keeping her voice low so that it would not carry through the thin tin walls of the trailer, "then I shall raise, I promise you, such a row as was never seen before. The law is the law, but it is supposed to protect this child, not persecute her. If Dr. Stirling dares set police on me and subjects this broken-hearted girl to any such brutal and bruising experience, I shall then fight him for her custody in every way I know." She panted heavily. "He will not dare," she said at last.

"Pearl?" Laila, lips parted, stood in the door. "May I? Please. It's so cosy and small . . ."

Pearl's face was grim. "As you wish, little darling," she said gently. "Come, then, in with you. Quickly. Be happy, Laila. I shall drive slowly."

Pearl closed the trailer's door. "One hour," she said to Estelle and cocked her head at her wrist-watch. "I wish no clash. Better, far better, to avoid a clash. We must not tear that child to pieces between us. But once I am away, they know not where, then the gauntlet is thrown. Do you see?" She didn't listen to Clive's answer, which barely came. "Yes, I shall go, peacefully, ostensibly alone, for the one hour. After that, when they know I have her, let them dare!"

Her heavy lids curled craftily. She glanced at the hitch between the trailer and the car. "Thank you very much, Mr. Breen. And au revoir."

Clive's feet shuffled. "I'm going to say I don't know anything about this. Mrs. Fleming will back me up, won't she?"

Pearl's eyes despised him. "We have not seen this man, Estelle," she said.

"No, dearest Pearl." A blank look came down over Mrs. Fleming's face, like a shadow falling. Then she was fluttering after Pearl.

"Ah, Pearl, bon voyage. And come safe home."

Pearl kissed her in benediction. She got into her coupé. Estelle had turned away, not to be too much affected by this parting. Laila was invisible, for the trailer windows were covered with slatted blinds.

Clive stood in the yard. Pearl stepped on the starter. It came over him what he was. He was a murderer! It came over him clearly that this was true, and furthermore, one person could prove it.

Laila could prove it. Her promise was based on her ignorance. She could and would and must prove his intent to let her die unless she did die . . . *unless she did die!*

He shouted, "Wait!"

Pearl waited. Clive started toward her and then he could not bear it. He ducked between the trailer and the car. "O.K." he called in a moment. "O.K. I was just checking."

Pearl bowed her head in grave farewell. Her house on her back, bound for the blue, she drove out into the alley, turned right, and was away.

Clive put his jumping hands in his pockets. He started back across the yard, not knowing where he was walking. He'd gone over a line.

All right. He *did* want her to die. He wanted that money. He had done his stupid best to see that she stayed lost until the poison worked.

But he knew she wasn't going to die. All his fumbling was stupid. He'd never get the money. He would be ruined. They would pick Pearl up. Laila would tell them how he'd put the car radio out of order. Laila would have to tell them that he knew about that urgent broadcast and, even so, he had helped her run away.

Clive groaned aloud. He hadn't cooked anybody's goose at all but his own.

Unless she did die!

Clive drew a shuddering breath. A flood of chancy hopes began to flow in his mind.

He had entered the house through the glass door. He saw Mrs. Fleming tilting her head in question and surprise. He started to stammer an excuse, to ask her permission to go through to the front door, when he saw Laila's hat and Laila's handbag on the couch.

He licked his lips. Going to be a murderer, he thought savagely, better take care of these loose ends. This Estelle — he tried to remember how Pearl had handled her. Finally, he said, "Pearl sent me to ask you to put Laila's things out of sight."

"Oh," she said. "Oh yes."

He watched her put them away in a table drawer. She seemed to have no idea why she acted. Her obedience was uncanny. He said, "May I go out at the front?"

"Oh yes."

"I wanted to thank you, Mrs. Fleming," he gushed, "for promising to forget that I was here. It's very good of you." Her eyes were so vague, she worried him. "You won't say I was here?"

"My promise to Pearl is sacred," and Estelle a trifle huffily. She stood with her eyes on a bowl of marigolds.

It occurred to Clive that she wasn't going to make the most impressive witness in the world. Anyhow, there was nothing he could do about her. Everything rode on the winds of chance. Everything about this whole business was catch-as-catch-can, somehow.

As he let himself out of the lady's front door, he was thinking of time. How many hours had gone already? It was three-thirty-five now. Mid-afternoon. If Pearl got away, and kept Laila away for the entire day tomorrow, it would probably do. He thought, if the stuff does get her, Pearl Dean will have some fun proving she didn't know thing about it.

A trifle comforted, he started off the tiny stoop. When he saw the cab, he thought, Luck. When Vince Procter leaned out of it and said, "Hey, buddy . . ." Clive knew the luck was bad.

"Yes?"

"What about that kid in the pink suit? What's your angle?"

Clive said stupidly, "What?"

"You heard me. What's the pitch? Anything in it for somebody like me?"

"I don't know what you are talking about," said Clive flatly. He simply did not know what else to say.

"Listen," said Vince, "this ain't a hospital, is it?"

Clive stared.

"Of course, I don't know if there is a reward . . ." Vince put on an evil leer, and waited for a reaction. When he saw there wasn't going to be any, he said, "O.K. I can always call Madison 7911."

"I don't know what you're talking about," said Clive angrily. (All he knew was that he dared not know.) "Do you want a fare?"

"So *you* don't know what I'm talking about?" said Vince. "O.K. As I say, I can always call in. Thought I'd see if you had any ideas, that's all. You got no ideas, buddy? Is that right?"

"I simply don't . . ." Clive froze. His voice dried up. Vanished, died, in the back of his throat.

". . . know what I'm talking about," finished Vince. "O.K. O.K. It won't do any harm if I call up, though." He felt frustrated. His little strategem hadn't paid off. This man wouldn't play, the way villains did in the movies. Vince slammed his cab into motion.

He was full of civic virtue, now. He was going to call

up, dump it on the police, and the heck with trying to detect anything.

The cab-driver went out of Clive's thoughts entirely. He was looking at the blue convertible that had turned the far corner and was sliding toward this kerb. He was frozen on *this* doorstep.

Here he stood, watching his red-haired cousin, Dee, and Andrew Talbot, tumble out and come pelting toward him.

Chapter Eleven

Dee flew up the short walk and Andrew Talbot came less impetuously after. Dee cried out her surprise to see Clive and Clive seemed paralysed with his own surprise to see them. It crossed Talbot's mind that Clive had made good time, had heard the news most promptly. What would he be doing here but looking for Laila? Dee made the same assumption, for she cried, "Clive, is she *here?*"

Clive said, "Gosh, I don't know, Dee. I just arrived . . ." and the motion of his hand said, couldn't they see, he had come in the cab.

Clive looked frightened. Dee was trying to smile at him. "Nothing bad is going to happen," she promised. She was heartened by having got here herself, at last.

How does she know nothing bad is going to happen thought Andy, even as her faith lightened the weight of his own fear, in contagion.

"We'll find her," Dee said. "Have you rung the bell?"

"Dee. this is awful!" Clive said with chattering teeth. "Listen, what hap — ?"

"How did you hear about it?" asked Talbot, coming up quietly. He was thinking, *we* were not so long delayed.

Clive jerked around. "I heard it on the air. I thought right away . . ."

"We all thought of Pearl Dean." Dee was pressing the bell with a firm finger. "She must be here." Dee yearned against the quiet door.

"Where's your car, Breen?" asked Andy.

"With the finance company," said Dee over her shoulder.

"Clive, did you go to the house?"

Clive's mouth opened and closed. He was jittery to the point of panic. He said, "No. No, I . . . Say, isn't anybody home?" And he began to push the bell.

"Coming," said Talbot calmly. "Stirling got the warning on the air pretty fast, didn't he?" Talbot felt vaguely something out of true.

Clive's mouth made a silent jawing and then the door opened. Estelle Fleming chirped. "Yes? What is it?"

"Oh, Mrs. Fleming," cried Dee. "Is Laila here?"

"Laila?" Estelle cocked her head sharply and tasted the name on pursed lips as if it were some strange fruit. Meantime, her eyes wandered over their faces.

Clive said, hoarsely, "My name is Clive Breen. My cousin and I are looking for Laila . . ."

Dee cut in impatiently. "I'm Dee Allison. Surely you remember me. I called you earlier . . ."

"Oh yes, Miss Allison," said Estelle, brightly. "And Mr. Breen, of course. Friends of Miss Dean. Yes, I remember. And Mr. . . ?"

"Talbot," said Andy. The woman was a type that irritated him. He knew at once that one had to try to communicate through a fog. No use to try for anything but a few brute facts. "Laila isn't here?" he demanded.

"But there is no one here but me, you know. Pearl has gone."

"Gone!" Dee said. "Where?"

"Oh, I never know where," said Estelle airily.

"How long ago?" asked Talbot quickly. Pound it out of her. Time and place. All you could hope for.

"Some time ago." Mrs. Fleming's head went sideways and she looked vague.

"It couldn't have been long ago," said Dee. "Pearl left our house at noon."

"She left a while ago," said Estelle with a hurt little frown. "I've been resting. I really . . ." She began to retreat from the doorway.

"Did she leave suddenly? Had she had a phone call?" pressed Andy.

"I don't . . . I really . . . I'm sorry . . ."

"You saw her go?"

"Of course I saw her go."

"May I use your phone?" said Andy briskly.

"Why, I suppose so." She stood aside doubtfully. "Won't you . . . come in?"

They walked into her house and her eyes fluttered as they passed her. Dee walked through the tiny foyer to the prim sitting-room across the front. Sunlight in the big glass porch across the back pulled her to stand in the wide opening to that place which was empty and silent.

Andy spotted the phone in the foyer and took it up quickly.

Clive came last. Andy, dialling the operator, looked back. He saw Mrs. Fleming cast upon Clive Breen a withering, angry, sharp and positive look. He gave Stirling's number. He pursued, in his mind, a fleeting wonder. Clive cleared his throat. "You mean to say that Pearl went off alone?" he said loudly.

"Dearest Pearl so often travels alone, you know," said Estelle evasively. She made a distortion of her mouth, meant to pass for a smile. "But she is coming back, of course." She nodded sharply three times. "Perhaps tomorrow." Andy frowned, sensing the evasion. But he had his party.

"Talbot, Doctor. From the Fleming house. Pearl Dean, has gone. Don't know where. Laila hasn't been here."

Stirling said, "Well, that's that, eh? Could they be meeting someplace?"

"Not unless there was a phone call. Laila doesn't use the

99

phone too readily."

"She might have, this time. Also, she might come there yet, you know."

"Yes, we'll take care of that."

"O.K. No news here. Three false rumours. Girls with long hair."

"Bound to be those," said Andy.

He forced the sickness out of his throat. No time for feelings of any kind. The head, the brain. No time to look at Dee's bright hair where the light was caught in that orange-gold. No time to feel for her, or be easy and gentle. Cut through everything to the facts of time and place until, under someoneunguessable stone, you'd find her, and be free of the guilt for your stupidity.

"What'll you do now? Wait there?" buzzed Dr. Stirling in his ear.

"If that seems best."

"Still the best bet," Stirling agreed. "Laila could have got confused, lost her way. Make it yet."

"Have you tried to check on taxicabs? Dee thinks . . ."

"Thought of that myself. Jonas Breen never took a bus in his life. I got on to as many cab companies as I could. Also got it on the afternoon news. Radio."

"How early?"

"Couldn't say. Why?"

"Never mind," said Andy. "How's Mrs. Vaughn?"

"Looks pretty serious, I'm sorry to say. Talbot, somebody better get that girl to me." He was matter-of-fact. The cry for haste screamed on the wire, just the same.

"Clive is here," said Andy suddenly.

"Is that . . . so?" said Stirling as close to a drawl as he ever came. "He ought to be helpful," he snorted.

"He . . . may . . . be," said Andy slowly.

"What's that?"

"I'll keep in touch, sir."

"What about Clive?" said Stirling sharply.

"Something a little odd about it," said Andrew Talbot. "I'll try to check, sir."

"Call me back."

Andy put the phone back thoughtfully. Speaking of probabilities, how probable was it that Clive took a cab all this distance in cousinly alarm? Came personally. He was not Dee. Dee would do everything personally if she could. But for Clive, it was a little . . . odd. Clive's panic was a little odd, too. It wasn't consistent with Clive's glossy surfaces. And why had this Mrs. Fleming given Clive that dirty look? There was a certain intimacy about a look as cross as that. One did not give a near-stranger, a man who had to tell you what his name was, quite such a glare. Or at least, if you did, there was something a little odd about it.

Dee had gone into the sun-room and was looking out at the garage and the bare lawn. Andy could see her. It seemed to him that she stood in an attitude of prayer, as if she were imploring the great sprawling city with its host of suburbs, the vast community of miles, of millions, frothing up the mountainsides nestling to the sea, dribbling off into the lowland valleys, to give her some clue.

Andy came sharply to the fact. "Mrs. Fleming," he said, "Laila Breen may come here yet and if she does . . ."

"Oh, she won't come here," said Estelle, somewhat too confidently. It was odd.

Dee turned around.

"But if she should," Clive took it up hastily. His voice had a tremor. "The doctor wants to get ahold of her."

"Doctor?"

Andy said loudly, "Yes, the doctor." But he knew she must be Pearl's disciple and the word might not have the same ring to her, the ring of integrity and command.

101

"It's important!" chimed Dee. "If she comes, you *must* call the hospital. I'll write the number . . ."

"Hospital?"

There was a word, too, corrupted in her mouth.

"She's been poisoned." Dee was bent over, writing.

"Why, how could she be poisoned?" said Estelle, almost merrily. "That's very strange."

"That's what the doctor says," Clive offered nervously. "The doctor wants to get her to the hospital. The doctor —" Clive licked his lower lip.

Talbot let himself stand there very quietly. It crossed his mind, now, that Clive's panic was a fact and must have a cause.

Clive looked as if he'd scream. He said shrilly, "We can't just stand here!"

Dee straightened and tore off the bit of paper.

Talbot said coldly, "Mrs. Fleming, if you are concealing something and it keeps us from finding Laila in time, the girl may die."

"That's so, Mrs. Fleming." Dee put the piece of paper in her hand. "That's really so." Dee blazed, as Andy was cold, in the same cause.

"Not really?" said Estelle vaguely. "How very strange!" She glanced down. "This is the number?" Her eyes were too sly. They glanced at her wrist-watch. Then she gazed at the marigolds. It seemed that they had settled into a tableau, there in the sun-room. Estelle watched the marigolds, and Andy watched her cocked head, the press of her lips in a half-smile, over secrets. Dee's blue eyes came puzzled and frightened to Andy's face.

But Clive flung himself across the room in long strides and back again as if he could bear no more of this. "Say," he blurted. "Dee . . . I've thought of something!"

"What, Clive? What?"

102

"Listen . . . Come here." He plunged across the room again and out through the glass door and Dee, caught by the mere motion, went after him.

Talbot was slower, but Talbot followed Dee.

In the backyard, Clive, gulping air, said to them, "Now look. If that Fleming is lying for Pearl you're not going to break her down. But why don't we see if anybody in the alley saw Pearl go off in her car? Could have seen Laila."

Dee cried, "Of course! Come on!" She started to run toward the alley and Clive hurried beside her. It was Clive who looked back. Andy was following.

Clive thought it was safe enough. There was no one in that alley, as far as he knew, and if there were, why, Laila had been hidden. So he moved without hesitation hurrying his cousin Dee along. He was giving them the illusion of progress and Dee, at least, had fallen for it. He was getting them away from that dizzy Fleming dame, who was willing to lie, perfectly willing. But she was a lousy liar and he didn't like the way Talbot turned quiet, and that Estelle was so vague she might tell the truth just by accident. She wasn't reliable. He couldn't bear any more of her. Clive rushed on.

Estelle was watching them through the glass. That dark quiet Mr. Talbot was the one who made her uneasy. Not what he had said, for she had been careful not to listen. But something in his manner, some unbendable thing she had met before. But she'd promised. Dear Pearl had been gone for not quite fifteen minutes and it wasn't time.

Clive, stumbling beside his red-haired cousin, felt as if he were caught in something as frantically confusing as a revolving door. Dee went flying down the alley, peering, snooping, at sedate little enclosures, quiet flower-beds, neat incinerators and cans of trash, looking for something alive.

At last, back of the three foot fence at the last residence before the shops along the cross street, they saw an elderly man puttering about the yard. Dee flung herself at the fence.

The old gentleman in his flowered shirt was happy to answer questions. Why, sure, he'd seen a car. Yep. Knew the lady. Big lady, always wore a black dress? Sure, he knew the one. Came along with her trailer and stayed up the block every once in a while.

Yep, saw her go, trailer and all and turn left on the street right there. Why, not more than a few minutes ago. He'd just put them calendulas in the ground.

Nope, nobody was with her that he saw.

Dee wailed, "She's not with Pearl! Where *could* she be? Where else could she go?"

"Here," Andy said quickly. "It may be only that she's missed Pearl. We better go back and wait in that house —"

"Wait?" Dee did not want to wait. Waiting was intolerable. She said so.

Clive Breen sagged against a post. He felt numb. He stopped listening to Dee's quick voice and Andy's quiet one. His mind moved sluggishly to the next problem. Better they didn't go back where that Estelle was. That was sure. She'd call up the Breen house when the hour was past, faithfully. But face that when it came.

He was seeing afar something moving into his future. When this was all over, there would be Estelle. She would know that *he knew* of the poison and had not seen fit to beg her to break her promise. Although he tried to push that distant menace out of his consciousness, his mind began to work on ways and means to counter it. He could say . . . He'd think of something he could say.

He knew already! He could say he hadn't known about the poison until the moment when that cabby told him.

Right there. Cover the cabby, too. So, terribly upset at what he had so ignorantly done, he had turned around to find Laila. If he had been tempted to cover up his frightening error, why, that was human. What did that matter, if he saved Laila. He could say . . . he could say *that* was his idea. *That* was why he'd brought them out here—to put them on the right trail without confessing that he knew, already, how right it was. It might cover everything. And leave him a fool and a coward but not a . . .

That is, it covered everything but Laila herself. It covered everything, *if Laila did die*. So he must be careful.

He could hear Dee pleading with Andy for something to do, and Andy arguing that it was sensible to wait here. Then Andy had her by the arm and Clive realized that he had to try to swing them, right now, away from Estelle, who lied so very badly. And then he saw it.

Through the alley's end he saw a cab, parked in sloppy haste with the door left open. He was absolutely sure what cab it was. His eye, moving over the façade of the shop before which the cab was standing, caught one sight only. A Bell Telephone sign. Now, calling the cops, as he had said he would, the cab-driver was in there. Clive straightened.

Couldn't hang around here with that driver to identify him and the cops coming to the Fleming house to split the whole thing wide open. It was as plain as two and two go together. Laila met Pearl, plus Pearl gone, equals cops after Pearl, equals Pearl caught and Laila found. And Clive in ruins. With that cab-driver to point his finger and say, "This is the very man."

There wasn't anything to do, anything to do, but tell some more of the truth to bolster up the story he was going to have to tell. Clive said loudly, "Hey, wait . . ."

"What, Clive? What?" Dee flashed around.

"Listen," his teeth chattered. "It just occurred to me.

105

Laila could have been in the *trailer*, couldn't she?"

"Oh!"

"Then she wouldn't have been seen."

"That's true!"

"True enough," said Andy slowly. "She could have been. That is, if Pearl didn't want her to be seen." He stood there, puzzling, frowning.

"Let's go!" cried Clive. He began to run. He raced at right angles, down the alley behind the shops, until he burst out into the street that ran before the Fleming house. He was sweating, pleading with Fate or whatever, to let them follow him once more. And they did follow. Dee was running, too.

Andy ran fastest of all. He raced ahead of Clive and blocked his way into the blue convertible. "Got to call Stirling on this. Wait here. I'll go back into Mrs. Fleming's phone."

But Dee cried, "Oh Andy, no. Not now. She's only minutes ahead of us. We can catch her."

"Of course we can," jittered Clive. "What do you want to delay for?"

"Where are you going?" said Andy coolly. "How will you turn? Which way to catch her without knowing her destination."

"But I do know," said Dee.

"That's impossible."

"Get in. Get in," yelped Clive. "Come on." He had to get *away*.

Andy got in as if he surrendered to a tide. Dee got into the middle and Clive on the outside. "Call the turns, Dee," said Talbot, sceptically, "if you think you know."

"Straight ahead, then left, and around . . ." She was panting. "They'll go to the shore, of course."

"It's a big ocean," Andy said grimly. But the car moved.

106

"Yes, but Pearl's got a pet place and it must be where she'll take Laila. Jonas and Laila and I drove down there once. I know where it is." Dee could see the place in her imagination. A tiny crescent of sand below cliffs, and the highway descended there, and roared on up to the cliff-tops, but you could turn into the cove. It was a place with a daemon for Pearl. Dee could feel the pull of it through Pearl's fibres.

If they went to the sea—and they would go to the sea because of Laila and her affinity—then they would go to this place and no other. She heard Clive asking shakily, "When was that, Dee?"

"Oh, you wouldn't know. You never wanted to bum around with Uncle Jonas as I did. Pearl's gone south, I'll bet."

"You're betting, all right," said Andy.

"Yes, and I think I know her route, too."

"You can't possibly . . ." Clive began, and stopped and swallowed.

"But I think I do. Pearl explained it to us. Andy, go on around this block and get on Rosecrans. Then east."

Andy said, amiably enough with just a trace of weary scepticism, "Call them in time, will you, Dee?"

"I'm trying to remember the back way she likes to sneak down there. It's just like Pearl. It's fruits and nuts."

"What?" She got a hard and almost angry look from Andy.

"Can I remember the order? First, I think it's Chestnut. Then I *know* it's a long back street called Lemon some-thing. Lemon Grove. Runs out into the country. Then Walnut, and then I think, Vineyard or Vineland. You come into the village of Orange. Then down through Tustin and Laguna Canyon."

"Fruits and nuts," said Andy. "La Pearl."

107

They were moving. The car proceeded, but Andy was not convinced. He was bound up in ideas of his own, other ideas. Dee herself felt so sure she was right that she pressed him.

"Andy, you do think Laila is with her in that trailer?"

"I think it's possible," he answered quietly. "Pearl *may* have lit out with her. She could be in the trailer. It's not likely — there are too many other possibilities."

"But we ought to catch Pearl *anyhow*."

"Yes," he admitted.

"It's so *close*," she said.

"If you're right about the fruits and nuts. Otherwise it's a tangent."

"I know. I know. But if she's *in* the trailer — then that Mrs. Fleming knew it and wouldn't tell us!"

"I think *that's* quite possible," said Andy. "I think there's something she didn't tell us. Don't you, Clive?"

Clive croaked, "Could be."

"Why would she do a thing like that?" Dee frowned.

"Because she promised," Clive said promptly and bit his tongue and tasted blood.

"Oh, I suppose so," said Dee sadly. "I suppose she would. That's . . . that's awful, really. I suppose Pearl doesn't know there's anything wrong with Laila."

But the notion shuddered into her head that Pearl Dean might know and arrogantly dismiss as modern nonsense the whole situation. Her heart curled in fright. Oh, it was true! Laila was wandering, not only in the maze that the city physically was, but the maze of the minds of the people . . . the criss-cross of ignorance and knowledge, the conflicts of opinion and personal objectives. People's loyalties and their limitations, the fits and starts of their motivations. This was the kind of haystack the needle was lost in.

Andy said, "Pearl can't know and go off with her. That's

what makes me doubt Laila's there. If she's there, she's hidden. *Why*, unless Pearl knows? But I can't believe even that fool woman—"

"Maybe Pearl doesn't believe it. She'd rather not, that I know." Dee began to try to say what she felt. "You have to figure from all *kinds* of points of view. Everybody Laila meets is being pushed by—whatever pushes the *kind* of person it is. It seems to me the lines cross and, and deflect—always do—and how we get through it at all—to wherever we're going . . ."

She gave up. Andy wasn't listening. At least he said nothing. She saw his mouth draw down at the corners. It was her cousin Clive who said hoarsely, surprisingly, "Yeah, it's catch-as-catch-can, all right."

They rode east, Clive rigid on Dee's right. On her left, Andy was far away. Ahead of them, perhaps, on this thread in the maze, there was Laila with the poison coursing secretly into her blood.

It seemed to Dee that something was dragging. "Hurry," she prodded.

"All this running around is no good, Dee," Andy said sternly. "All this guessing. Better to go back and pound what she knows out of that Fleming dame. It's even better to use the telephone."

"Straight on. Keep going." Dee's foot pressed the floor.

"That's your way," he said almost absent-mindedly. "Straight on, keep going. Take care of it personally. But I'm afraid . . ."

"What would you do?" Clive said belligerently.

"Stop and think."

"I'm thinking." Dee put her hands to her head. "I'm thinking all the time."

"Stop, eh?" said Clive. "Well, she's not your cousin."

"No, she's not my cousin," Andy said. "I've thought of

109

that."

Clive said, nervously, "Fruits and nuts. I don't know, Dee. It sounds crazy."

"It's not crazy," Dee insisted. "It's rather a good way to remember. Pearl's way. She must be so close . . ."

Andy glanced at her face. The time was four p.m. He said, grimly, "All right. We'll take a crack at chasing her. It's possible we can catch Pearl, at least. Which way?"

"Straight on. Why don't you believe Laila's with her?" asked Dee.

"I've been thinking," he said, and said no more.

Chapter Twelve

Laila sat on the broad bed built into the rear of the trailer. Everything around her was clattering and rattling. She seemed to jump and rattle and chatter within herself. The little enclosure was far from the cosy comfort it had seemed to promise. The trailer was not designed for smooth riding but for standing still.

At least she was hidden. No one could see her. No one could find her. No one would recognize her clothes or her hair. No one would seize her and carry her back to Dr. Stirling or Dee or Andrew.

So she endured the vibration and the bouncing, but it was doing strange things to the hurt in her heart. She couldn't lie down and weep into Pearl's pillow. There was no stillness in which her grief could flow. The luxury of concentration upon her woe was impossible because of the clatter. She had bitten her tongue twice already. Laila pushed her long hair up from her ears.

She had a memory of herself as a small girl, having a tantrum and being grasped and shaken out of her temper into a mode of common sense. It seemed to be happening again.

She tried to wedge herself to a more stable position. She had begun to feel the least bit seasick . . . and much more sensible. She could not weep so Laila began to think.

Why was she here, enduring so uncomfortable a journey? To be with Pearl? But she wasn't with Pearl. She had hidden herself back here where she couldn't talk to Pearl or receive the petting and the sympathy she craved. Why had she hidden herself?

So that Dee and Andrew couldn't find her?

But Dee and Andrew only wanted to know where she was. Laila was to blame for that. It was *not* wrong of them to worry. And Dee would have let her go to the sea with Pearl, had Laila told her about it. Dee wouldn't have tried to force her to come back. No, she was hiding from Dr. Stirling. It was the doctor who was trying to force her to come back.

But oh, she was being shaken and jolted right out of a silly baby tantrum.

Why should she be afraid to go back to the hospital? She didn't want to go, She didn't think she needed to go, but she was silly to feel afraid. Dr. Stirling had no reason to wish to hurt her. She was being shaken into facing the truth about Jonas, too.

Dr. Stirling had not hurt Jonas, either. Or, at least, Laila did not really think so. If she had believed it, she would have told someone long ago and let them lock her in, somewhere, if that was what followed. Because you did not allow people to kill people and say nothing. So it wasn't a real belief, even, but a bogeyman by which she tantalised herself with fear. Something, sure enough, that she didn't understand. But if you did not know, why then, you did not know. It wasn't sensible to say it must be something horrible and terrible, because I do not know. Now, shrewdly, she remembered Clive, pronouncing quickly that long queer word. Hypo . . . something. To him there was something familiar about that word. She did not think it had frightened Clive, at first. But then later . . . ? Her mind turned back.

The truth was she didn't like Dr. Stirling because he always said "Nonsense". Maybe it often *was* nonsense. It was silly to pretend she thought he was a wicked man.

The shaking continued. Dr. Stirling was not wicked and he was not trying to scare her, cruelly. Why then had that voice come out of the radio and asked for people to watch for her and send her to the hospital? Because she *was* ill, as it had said? She was not. Perhaps Dr. Stirling thought she was ill, for some mistaken reason. Well, then, all she had to do was announce her blooming health to him. She wasn't a bit ill, really.

Suppose she were? Pearl did not know what they were saying about her; Pearl hadn't the least idea of illness in her mind. Pearl was being so good and kind. Laila concluded it wasn't very fair. It wasn't right. It wasn't good. If you *trust* a person, you don't *fool* her, do you?

Unsure, uneasy, Laila got herself off the bed and stumbled through the narrow place between cupboards into the forward section of the trailer. Clive had been kind but not so very wise. She'd better signal to Pearl, some way. She would tell her about the voice on the radio, because Pearl was truly trying to help her, and it was not fair. Laila was sure, now, that she and Clive together had made a silly mistake. It was even worse than a mistake. It was a kind of lying. There were twisty things about Clive that she sensed, now. Dishonest, not brave. Perhaps he had meant to be kind, but they should have been honest with Pearl.

She lifted the blind across the front and she waved and tapped the glass, but Pearl didn't or couldn't see. Laila could see Pearl's big head, unturning, and the solid set of Pearl's shoulders. They trundled on.

Laila touched the door handle. When Pearl stopped the car, as she must from time to time, why then Laila would get out and run forward. But the door seemed to be locked. At least, she couldn't get it to open.

Jiggle, jiggle, joggle. All the flesh on her bones was

bouncing. She stumbled to look into the tiny mirror over the little sink. Her blurring image shook before her shaken eyes. Maybe she wasn't so very well. Laila rode there in all the rattle and bounce and her mind was thrown into rackety confusion. She staggered to the broad upholstered seat built into the trailer's nose and fell upon it.

She did not *believe* that Mamma's love was alive again in Pearl Dean. It was not the same. Mamma had been one to sing and play and dream, but she had been clever, too. Who was it who had shaken Laila when she was little and spoken tartly when it was necessary? "Come, come, where are your bones?" Pearl was soft, soft all through. But Mamma, like grandmother, had bones, and was kind and yet true. As Andrew had been true, even if what he had said had hurt her feelings. Clive was a boneless one! Clive helped her to *deceive*. But she thought Dee was true! And Dr. Stirling was bony and thorny and she was a little bit afraid of him, but he could be one who was true, after all.

The blue convertible hurtled on. They were running east and south, through an industrial section, fleshless places. Then they were once more in a realm of multitudes of houses, the old jumbled, the new serried in accurate ranks, all lying in the open sunshine of the flat land, all able to see on this smogless afternoon, the blue hills north, the black lattice of oil wells between them and the seaward horizon.

Dee was not certain of this part of Pearl's route. They had found no Chestnut. She was afraid it might have been Cherry. But she was sure that they must work past the beach cities on an inland street called Lemon Grove.

Andy was following her directions in silence, now, while Clive bothered her ears with doubts and alternatives. Andy was calm and obedient and yet disapproving. Clive was nervous and unnerving and argumentative. Dee's hopes were tinged with doubt and foreboding as they went spinning block after block and never, on the way ahead, caught sight of Pearl's aluminium. When Andy said, again, "Dee, we ought to stop this chasing and call back," she was almost ready to agree.

But Clive yelped, "And lose time? No, no, that'll take too much time! We'll lose our chance—"

"We're lost, as it is."

"Not yet," said Dee, strengthened in her conviction. "No, not yet. Pearl will be on Lemon Grove."

"Why can't I make you see it would be much more sensible to call Stirling . . . let him get Pearl picked up. And be quicker that way."

"What's quicker about it?" Clive said argumentatively. "We can't be far behind her."

"Can't we?" said Andy. "Pearl may be halfway to Santa Barbara. Or in Big Bear by now, for all we know."

"Scare the poor kid to pieces," said Clive bitterly. "Sirens and stuff. Cops. You're wanted. And all that. Gosh, I don't like to think of what it'll do to Laila." His eyes swivelled to his Cousin Dee. In his double act, he had to keep pushing. He hoped they'd quarrel.

"Andy," said Dee quietly, "I *am* going on a real probability."

Andy said, "Nuts to probability. I take a certainty when I can get it. I'm stopping at the next phone booth. This is ridiculous."

Dee cried, "Don't stop."

"I'm going to call. This is a job for the cops."

"Scare her to death," said Clive again.

"Don't be such a fool," snapped Andy. "I'll risk scaring her to death. That stuff she's got in her will kill a lot surer than fright can. Dee, don't you know I'm right?"

She said, "If she's with Pearl, then I know where they'll most probably go."

"If," he said, "and that's a big one. I think I've been indulging your instinct to rush around. Sorry, but I've got to do the best I know. I'm thinking of Laila."

Clive was mouse-quiet. Let them fight, he thought, complacently.

Dee said, "So am I. I think this is so probable, I've got to go on *this* thread. All right, Andy, you stop. You call. Let me go on."

"With the car?" he said.

"Yes, I'll need the car."

"And I?"

"You can phone," she said. "We interfere with each other anyhow. I'm a handicap to you. We don't agree. Maybe you can find her your way."

"I'll find her," he said savagely, "anybody's way. All ways. There's a phone." He sent the car swerving and squealing on to the apron of a gas station and stopped it. He got out. "Come along," he said sternly. "I want you to describe that car and trailer."

"No, no. We're on Pearl's heels. We can't *wait!*" She was looking up into his stern face that had aged, already, in this one afternoon. "Oh, be free of me," she cried, "and let me go. You know I will find her for you if I can." She was blind with sudden tears.

Clive caught them both unawares. He stood up and forced his body over and around Dee into the driver's seat. "She's right," he yammered. "We're going on."

"Wait a minute . . ." Andy clung to the car. He said rapidly, "Dee, leave if you want to. I won't make you go my way. But I must tell you, you're not on the right track. I think Clive knows it."

"What!"

116

"There's something funny going on. He got us out of there too fast. He's got us on a chase and we don't *know* Laila is in that trailer. I don't think it's his guess. I think it's his purpose."

"You're wasting time," Clive yelped. "Now you're deliberately wasting time."

"We can't waste time," said Dee, bewildered.

"Dee," Andy's face was dark with the darkness of his thought. "Don't you know that if Laila should die . . ."

"She's not going to die. I won't *let* it happen."

"Think about what pushes other people. *He* would," said Andy. "*He* might. Clive might . . . let it happen for a nice profit."

"Andy!" Dee was utterly shocked. "*Nobody* would let it happen. You don't mean that!"

His grey eyes were sorry.

"She's my cousin, too," cried Dee.

"Yes, I know," he said. "I just don't like it. I'm not trying . . ."

Clive said, "He's trying to waste time and that's all he's doing. Look out!" He yanked Dee down into the seat.

"Wait! Dee!" Talbot grabbed for the ignition key, too late. Then he tried to leap aboard. But the blue convertible spurted up and Clive shoved viciously with his elbow. Dee turned, knee on seat, and saw Andy catch his balance on the very brink of a fall and then run a few futile steps. She saw an attendant running to his side as the car lurched out into traffic and Clive slammed it ahead.

Clive said furiously, "This makes better sense than listening to his insults. We can't be far behind. You and I agree. We mustn't waste the time. We've got to keep going."

She faced around forward. Her hair whipped her cheek. In a very disagreeable painful way, it made sense to keep going without Andy. She meant it with all her heart, what she had said. She would find, for her love, the girl he loved. For the first time, she realized that she too was Laila's heir. She realized Andy had thought of it. It seemed all wrong to have thought of such a thing. She thought, "I don't know him. Nor does he know me. Nor ever shall we." She put her bare hand in the sun, where the wind would weather it. It was twenty-six minutes after four.

Talbot stood, biting his cheek. The attendant seemed angrier than he. "I seen that," he offered. "You want a car? You want to chase them?" He was hot and furious.

"Not I," said Andy. "I want some change. I want to telephone." His voice was cold and controlled.

"That was a fine thing for him to say," Clive snorted. "You know who profits."

"What do you mean, Clive?" Dee said impatiently, holding herself steady and watching the street signs. Clive was a wretched driver.

"I mean we both profit. You, too, Dee. If Laila . . ."

"Don't even . . ." she flared around at him.

"I didn't start this. *He* did. O.K. Listen, Dee, money never crossed your mind, I suppose, but remember . . . Talbot got engaged to you while he had reason to believe *you* were Uncle Jonas's heir."

"He didn't even *know* about Uncle Jonas. Don't be so silly."

"You *think* he didn't. You remember all that noble speechmaking the night after Jonas died? Yeah. But who wanted to *hear* about the will?"

"Oh, Clive, please. What's money got to do with it? Who's thinking of money?"

"Your boy friend," snarled Clive. "Obviously, he's thinking of money."

"That's not true," she said weakly.

"No? What's he mean, 'profit,' then?"

"I don't know," said Dee. "I don't care."

"Listen, Dee . . ."

"We've got to go right."

"What?"

"Clive, you're in the wrong lane."

"I'll get over. Take the next one." Clive got himself well tangled in the traffic. "You're only thinking about Laila," he proclaimed, "and I'm only thinking about Laila. You don't imagine *he* ever did any thinking about Laila?"

"Clive, please. Work over into the right lane. You're not . . ."

"I am. So all right. She's nuts about him, poor little bunny. He could marry Laila and the whole damn fortune any day he said the word. You think he hasn't been tempted?"

Dee said, "Clive, be quiet."

"Maybe he's been tempted," Clive insisted. "But nobody wants to look like such a heel as to throw you over for the girl who's got the money. This is different — kind of opportunity."

"Clive, I don't want to hear . . ."

"You heard *him*, didn't you? Implying I'd just as soon let her stay lost until she dies, so I'd get the money. All right. Now you can hear me. If she stays lost and dies, he marries the same money. Doesn't he?"

"No."

"Yes, he does. He marries you. And a half of the money. You'll sure be a lot better off financially than you are now."

"Clive, you're so wrong. And that's the meanest . . . the smallest, meanest . . ."

"All right," Clive snarled. "But who wants to stop and call back, all the time? Who gets in an argument and makes a delay? Who doesn't look like he's so crazy to catch Laila?"

Dee's eyes shot sparks. "I never heard such a horrible idea in my life. *Nobody* would do a thing like that."

"Where you been, Dee?" said Clive sadly. "Not around."

"I think you're disgusting!"

They whipped on. Around to the right. Cars ahead, blue, green, yellow and black. Nothing shining. No trailer. No Pearl. Clive was sweating. He couldn't figure out a way to blow a tyre or pull a wire somewhere and stop this pell-mell flight into disaster. He'd thought it not a bad idea to get rid of Talbot. He was glad to be in the driver's seat. Maybe he'd think of a way, yet. Clive was afraid his cousin, Dee, who maddeningly knew so much, had put them on the right trail. His mind twisted and squirmed. He couldn't afford to catch them. But he had to *seem* to be hell-bent to catch them. That Talbot, the crust of the things he'd said. So Clive had to muddy the waters. He couldn't stop talking.

"You know, Dee," he said plaintively, "what you want to realise is that he's human. It doesn't *seem* exactly criminal, just to hold up a little bit. Keep talking about doing the sensible thing. Let her get lost, eh? I mean, he may not think it all out, but, you know, subconsciously . . . What I'm trying to say, that could happen."

"Oh, stop it," she cried. "Stop that and drive. Or let me drive."

Clive clamped his teeth. She wouldn't stop watching the road. She wouldn't let him stray. She wouldn't get upset over Talbot and the money. She was on the right trail. She'd never give up. He couldn't shake her. He couldn't muddle her. He couldn't stop her.

He hated her!

Chapter Thirteen

Pearl Dean was one of the worst drivers in the world. She thought she was cautious. But she was sluggish in her reactions and vague in her purposes. She was out of phase with everything on the highway. A multitude of crisp and skilful decisions on the part of other drivers saved her from disaster about once in every mile.

Now, she trundled along in her erratic way, varying her speed with her mood, sometimes confident enough to step up to forty miles an hour, sometimes drifting hesitantly in a zigzag across lanes. She liked to drive to music but she could find no music this afternoon. The radio seemed to be out of order. So she fell alternately from a drifting daydream to a sudden alarmed nervousness and the little car went as her moods went, and the trailer after it.

Pearl preferred back ways to fast through streets, perhaps because she herself was less of a nuisance on these. So she wound and trundled her caravan through quiet residential sections, but she could not avoid all the through streets, all the business sections, or all the traffic signals. Pearl was not one who always saw a red light quickly enough to incorporate it into her plans. Now, as she trod on the brake and came to a stop with the coupé blocking the pedestrian crossing, she peered about her. She realised she was getting out of the city. Soon she would be on her pet street, her own way south, and beyond the city limits and the province of the Los Angeles Police Department.

Pearl relaxed. Her mind went ahead to her destination. The sea. The darling cove. The sea sounds and the lonely peace. She threw herself into the self-hypnosis she enjoyed.

A loud voice was coming from somewhere near. The news, on somebody else's radio. Absent-mindedly, Pearl fiddled again with the knobs of her own. Too bad. Ah well, she had a little portable, back in the trailer. She and Laila could have music this evening, to the sea's chorus. They would watch the high stars and Pearl could talk and talk and the child would listen, delightfully.

Pearl had been drawn to Jonas Breen, yes, truly drawn. The man had excited her and she knew she had entertained him. He was one of the very few mature and intelligent persons willing to sieve from her potpourri of notions the grains of enlightenment. For Jonas's sake, she would soothe and protect his darling child, who was Pearl's own, by Pearl's reckoning. Who was in danger because of the wicked money. Who must marry and bear a child to be safe from the danger that was entwined with the money. Who must have love and had Pearl's. . . .

The woman dreamed on . . . until the light changed and somebody honked and prodded her ahead.

Behind her, Laila, crumpled on the couch, was holding her ears. The loud voice had penetrated and shaken the thin walls of the trailer. Her name. Her own name. All over the city, everywhere, people were hearing it. "Caucasian. Eighteen years of age. This girl has been poisoned. Anyone seeing this girl, please call Madison 7911. Or take her at once to Greenleaf Hospital. Please notify Madison 7911. This girl has been poisoned."

Poisoned?

Now, Pearl knew what they were saying. Pearl was right beside that loud voice . . . could not help but hear it. So she would soon come and open the door and at last tell Laila what to think, whether to believe, what to do, what to do. . . . A very bitter truth had come to Laila Breen. She couldn't think for herself, not yet, because she did not know enough.

Oh, how could she be poisoned? Mrs. Vaughn must be the one who had been poisoned. Maybe they were confused about that, some strange way. And maybe not. But Pearl was her friend, and Pearl knew more than she, and Pearl would do what was best to do, now that she had heard the radio.

The trailer lurched forward. The jiggling, the rattling, the relentless journey began again.

Talbot put his coins in. Stirling's voice was rough and quick in his hear. "Talbot? Say, the police got a tip from a cab-driver who says he picked Laila up. She was not alone. She was with a man. He took them to Flemings."

"When?" Talbot staggered. His suspicion grew hot.

"That's the question. Whether before or after you got there, we can't . . ."

"Did the police go to Flemings?"

"On their way. Should be there now."

"A man, eh?" said Andy. "Any description of this man?"

"Nothing very distinctive. Tall. Brown hair. Grey eyes."

"Clive?" said Andy.

He heard Stirling's gasp. "Nothing to contradict the idea of Clive," the doctor said. "Why? What do you . . ."

"I'm puzzling my head about cousin Clive. I got the

idea he was in it somehow. Don't ask me why. The Fleming woman was lying. And he knew it. He was damn nervous, watched her like a hawk, got us out of there, ran us out on what he says is Laila's trail. I've been wondering if it is the real trail. Are the police trying to pick up Pearl Dean?"

Stirling said, "I suggested it. Right after you told me she had gone. Thought we ought to check with her. But tell me this, because I don't know. What does she drive?"

"Old car, small. A coupé. Black. Chevvy, I think. Can't swear to that. And she's hauling a trailer."

"I didn't know that. What's it look like?"

"I don't know that, sir." Andy groaned.

"Ask Dee. Dee's probably seen it."

"Dee's not with me." Andy's voice was tight.

"Where is she?"

"Gone with Clive. Chasing Pearl. In my car. Look, who knows about this? Who can I contact in the police department?"

"Name's Sweeney." Dr. Stirling gave a number. "Why?"

"I want that cab-driver," Andy said. "I'm stranded. I need a cab and what I need even worse is the driver who will know that man again."

"Clive, eh?" said Dr. Stirling, remotely on the far wire. "Well, it's hard to believe. But say, try the Fleming house. It's quite possible the driver is *there*. Talking to the police."

"O.K."

"Talbot. Hey, Talbot. Is Dee all right?" The doctor listened to the dead phone. He was a man of logic. He did not jiggle the phone and futilely flash the operator. He hung up, instead.

He said out loud, "That Clive is a moral idiot but even he . . . Dammit," he said to his secretary, "stick on that phone, Mary. She's gone too long. I don't like the way this looks. If somebody *sets out* to hide her, that's going to be different. That's not the same problem, damn it. Get me that Sweeney again."

"Yes, Doctor."

"That Pearl Dean! Who knows . . . ?"

Talbot was calling the Fleming number. He thought, poor Dee. I already know much more than she, from the telephone. He winced, thinking of Dee's tears. God damn it, why couldn't you keep your balance between those two girls? He sneered at himself. You damn fool. When this is over, leave town.

Clive was still chewing sourly on his theme. "So Talbot's the one who gave her something to run away about, eh?"

"Clive, watch the road."

"That's interesting, too. Did he know she ate that stuff? Talbot, I mean."

"No, no of course he didn't. He didn't know anything about it when he talked to her."

"Didn't? Couldn't have overheard . . . ?"

(Overheard? Dr. Stirling at the telephone, barking his medical terms. Andy used them sometimes. Andy used a term like *greenstick fracture*. Andy could have overheard and understood. Dee played with the possibility and then smiled over it.)

"Don't be silly, Clive. Suppose he had? He still did not know *she* had eaten any. Nobody knew it until Sidney told us. Clive, let me drive?"

"Nuh, uh." Clive accelerated. "Listen. Laila knew what she ate, I guess. Maybe he asked Laila?"

"He couldn't have," said Dee calmly.

"He could have," Clive snapped, "but you're too stubborn to consider it."

"I think you must be crazy," she said wearily. "First you want me to consider that Andy wanted to marry Laila. Then, that he's trying to murder her. Choose one."

"He could have wanted first one and then the other," Clive whined. "I'm just wondering. After all, none of us know very much about Mr. Andrew Talbot. Anybody can work in an office. How do you know how his mind works?"

"I'm beginning to know," said Dee hotly, "an awful lot about how *your* mind works, and it isn't decent. It makes me sick."

"You're sure of him, aren't you? You can't see that he's got a motive."

Dee let her head tip back. "I've got the motive. I'd get the money, wouldn't I? I should be jealous of her, too."

Clive's mouth fell open. Dee went on:

"You're not very bright, Clive. Don't you see the ring I'm not wearing? Don't you know when we find her and she's safe, Andy will want to take care of her, for evermore?"

"Do you mean . . . ?"

"You can't tell me Andy's trying to hold back. Why are you trying to tell me such a . . . ?"

Clive said, a little breathlessly, "Dee, do you mean that if she lives, you've lost him?"

"Of course, I've lost him," cried Dee. "Either way. And what has that got to do with it? What you call motives are nonsense, Clive. I'm telling you because I know. Nothing can stop me from trying to find her. So hurry. Turn left at the next corner. That will be Lemon Grove."

Clive chewed his cheek. He turned left. Now they were on a street called Lemon Grove.

Chapter Fourteen

The mists that blew in the mind of Pearl Dean swirled and changed. Although she had been absent, in a dream, her ears had recorded well enough what went on about her. Now she heard a playback. It came to her, all that loud voice had been saying. Laila's name and description. The situation she was in.

She sat, massive, with her fat foot frozen on the accelerator. The car moved on, but now the noble dome of Pearl's forehead wore a crease of stern reflection. It was nearly five o'clock. She was well out of the city. She wanted to keep the course she was on. Oh, she wanted to. Her dream of herself as the comforter, the guardian, the proxy mother was strong, but Pearl had run into some kinds of trouble before. The way of discretion rose like a rock in her path. She felt briefly resentful. She had been deceived, somehow. But there was no doubt in her mind about what she must do.

Her eyes began to roll and take in the geography. She was on Lemon Grove, which, here, was narrow and ran between fields in open country. The next crossroad was far ahead. She remembered it. A gas station there and a country store, a few dwellings, a cluster of buildings on the four corners. She must turn to her left on the crossroad and go quickly. . . .

Her head began to ache, jolted by the sharp incursion of reality, calling for such sudden real action. Nervously her foot pressed down. The little car responded. The trailer jerked and followed.

Far behind, the blue convertible rolled over a rise.

"There she *is!*" cried Dee. "There she is! Oh, Clive! Oh, good for us! Now, catch her!"

Clive felt the perspiration trickle on his back.

"I'll try," he said virtuously. He said, "Dee, I wish you were a little more open-minded. You see everything black and white. I mean, people are human. Nobody's perfect. You've got to take that into consideration . . . *You've* got a conscience. *You* think everybody . . ."

"Don't talk now!" cried Dee. "Just hurry!"

"I'll hurry," he said viciously. He hated his cousin Dee. Girl scout, he thought. "Don't worry. I'll hurry." He tramped on the gas and the car surged and roared forward.

There were eye-witnesses to what happened at the crossroads at five o'clock that Wednesday afternoon. The police, combining this testimony with a study of the skid marks later, were able to work it out quite plainly.

As far as the blame could be assigned, the coupé did wrong twice over, passing the man with the flag, then turning left against the light. The blue convertible was going too fast and had also failed to see the flag or red light. The red panel truck coming forward at right-angles to traffic had been under the flag's protection. It was not to blame, but it had made the south-west corner a blind one, just the same. Then, the Buick coming south on Neptune Road had not been able to stop. His brakes were questionable.

It all added up to a mess.

The four corners exploded. People seemed to be blasted out of the store and the houses. They came like popcorn out of an empty-looking pan. In minutes, an ambulance screeched up from the south and police cars wailed in from north and west.

A witness who saw it all from the beginning was old Mrs. Gilman. Seated in her wheel-chair on the porch of her house on the south-east corner, she had a box seat. Oddly enough, it did not shock her. She saw it happen with a kind of savage revengeful satisfaction, although right afterwards, of course, she felt sorry. But it brought to her a vivid remembrance of the last time she had felt alive. Two years ago. Just before her personal crash.

That, too, had been an accident at a crossroads, just such a sudden tangle of metal and flesh. In it she had lost both her feet at the ankles and received a slash across her neck which had done its damage. Ever since, she could neither walk nor speak. She hadn't been quite alive, since then.

Now her dumb throat ached to scream, but the scream would have been tinged with a triumphant "See! It can happen to you, too! See! That's how it was! That is what comes of your speed and your carelessness, you silly people!"

It was just as well, she knew a moment later, that she couldn't scream, for it wouldn't have been becoming in a gentle old woman to scream in such a manner. She devoted herself to feeling sorry for those injured people, as sorry as only she could be, and to watching everything in sight from her position in the porch. She was glad that she had made her attendant, housekeeper, and practical nurse, Agnes Nilsson, bring her out and settle her here so early. She knew about what was scheduled to happen at seven o'clock across the street, and she had intended to enjoy that spectacle from its slightest beginnings. That was how she came to have a balcony seat for this unscheduled excitement.

Agnes, who fancied herself as a nurse, forgot all about
Mrs. Gilman, temporarily, and went right down into it to
see what she could do to help. So Mrs. Gilman, rather
glad to be forgotten, was able to watch a good deal of what
was happening. Not everything. A linen service truck
had slewed to an angle and stopped smack in the intersection and it blocked her view of the goriest bits. For this she
was not sorry. She was not really a bloodthirsty old lady.
Just lonely and unfortunate and not altogether alive, any
more.

Mike Torres, the driver of this linen service truck, told
his swamper, Frank Turner, to stay with it, and he went to
help. A couple of workmen rushed out of the Baxter
house on the south-west corner and into the mêlée. The
men at work unloading a truck marked KROV on the
margin of the Baxter property stood and exchanged ejac-
ulations. Men from the gas station on the north-west corner jumped to stop traffic before somebody else piled up.
The police soon had the four feeding roadways blocked,
and things simmered down. Slowly, in jabber and cry, all
was disentangled. It became clear what had happened.

The light had been red for those running east and west.
The red panel truck needed to be manoeuvred into a position close to the front façade of the Baxter house. A man
with a red flag had seized this chance when traffic before
the house was not flowing, and he had stepped into the
road to flag down and stop the east-bound cars before
they reached the crossroads. The red truck had been nos-
ing directly across the road, when the old Chevvy coupé
pulling a house trailer had come speeding and rocking
east and missed seeing the flag. It had rocketed around
the red truck's nose and just as it did so, a blue convertible
racing as if it meant to overtake and pass had taken the

same sudden twist around the outraged red truck on which the driver had slammed the brakes. A Nash, scooting north with the green light and on the proper side of the road, had been startled to a fast and clever dodge when the old Chevvy coupé had come fast out from behind the mask of that panel truck.

The Nash, unable to stop, had looped swiftly. But the coupé, intending a left turn against traffic, but finding itself on the wrong side of the road too close to that Nash, had in panic and confusion taken a second wild swerve. So that, although the Nash skinned by safely, the coupé had been yanked around almost into a U turn and the blue convertible had hit the coupé nearly head on. At the same moment, the Buick, coming legally south on Neptune, also hit the coupé which had taken this sudden fishhook turn into its path.

Besides all this, the quick turns and immediate impact of the coupé with two cars had sent its trailer reeling. Loose of its hitch, it had skidded and gone sailing across the intersection, waltzing in front of the linen service truck, which had been following the Nash, heading north. By a whisker and a lurch, the linen truck had escaped being hit, and the trailer turning a full circle on its own axis had trembled to a stop, upright, close to Mrs. Gilman's low wire fence on the south-east corner.

At the bottom of the trouble, the red panel truck, which was nevertheless innocent, legal, flag-protected, had suffered a bent bumper and shattered headlights where the convertible's tail had caught it.

The man with the flag had a terrible blood-chilling suspicion that he had suddenly become invisible and he could not stop stammering out his righteousness and the fact that he had done his full duty.

Now, of course, cars coming east piled up behind the

blue convertible. Cars coming north piled up behind the barrier of the stalled linen service truck. Cars coming south were falling in line behind the Buick and cars coming west were blocked by the Nash and the general confusion.

It was a mess.

Only the ambulance could get a clear way in, on the left side of the north-bound road, for there were injuries and it was needed. A woman in that coupé. Girl and man in the convertible. Driver of the Buick wasn't feeling too well, either.

Mrs. Gilman, chained to her chair, was almost the only one who could clearly see the side door of that aluminium trailer. Miz Paget came and ran her two children away from there in maternal anxiety for their sensibilities, and the attention of everyone else was riveted, of course, on the central drama and the injured people. But Mrs. Gilman saw the door of the trailer quiver. It seemed to have been warped and sprung. She saw it open. It seemed to her that the girl who got out and stepped over the bashed-down wire fence into the margin of her own lawn was an apparition, for she had a great unfashionable mass of dark hair down her back. Her face was small and white and lovely as a wax doll.

Laila was dizzy. She was not hurt at all. The waltz of her little prison had not thrown her anywhere except against the soft upholstery where she had been lying. All that had happened was that the door had sprung. So she got out.

She had kicked off her pumps long ago. She stood in her stocking feet on the good ground with her shoes in her hand. She saw the old lady, up on the porch, straining forward in the chair, but the old lady did not speak or call to her. The bulk of the trailer hid the crossroads from

132

Laila's sight, but she could hear the talk and noise. There must be a great many people around the other side of the trailer. She heard the sirens swooping in. The mechanical wailing frightened her. She braced herself by her hands on the aluminium side.

What she had better do, she did not know. Finally, she began to stumble slowly to her right and she came slowly around the trailer's end.

Frank Turner was standing high on a ledge at the back of the linen service truck, so that he could see into the heart of things. He could see Mike Torres helping them get a woman out of that coupé, working right along with the men off the ambulance. He felt proud of his boss. He felt good about it. Mike was kinda strict and grumpy, but when it came to something like this, he was a real good guy.

Frank himself was not long out of Korea and kind of tentative about what he did, because he had a hunch that he'd be going back. His knee didn't incapacitate him much, that he could see. Anyhow, he'd lost his steam about jumping into a job to get himself on the way to riches. He didn't care so much any more, about that. He'd come home with the gift of being wholeheartedly where he was, of tasting everything gentle and sunny and peaceful while it touched him, and enduring all that was not, without flinching. He was new on this job and obedient in a soldierly manner. So he stuck to the truck and his young face with the hollowed places at the temples, the thin drawn cheeks, the boy's mouth and the man's eyes, was serious but calm.

Something made him turn his head and he looked around and there was an angel.

Chapter Fifteen

She was wearing a long blue coat, standing right there below him, and her pale lovely face was tipped up, and that hair! Man, this was something different! This wasn't any bobby-soxer.

She said, "What is it? What is everyone looking at?" in a sweet clear voice.

He thought she lived around here. He said, "Kind of a bad accident, Ma'am. Some people got hurt, I'm afraid."

"Is Pearl hurt?"

(Just as if he'd know who Pearl was.) "I don't know, Ma'am," Frank said, smiling at her. He jumped down. He said, "You look kinda pale, Ma'am. Some friend of yours was in a car, you think? Is that it? And you're afraid . . . ?"

"Yes, that's it," said Laila gravely. "Yes, I . . . I am afraid."

"Well," Frank said, "what can I do? Look, would you want to climb up and see if you can see? I could open the doors," Frank said eagerly and he reached up and did so.

Now there was more than a ledge. There was a full step revealed and he helped her up on it. Some of her hair fell across the flesh of his hand. It was soft. It was beautiful, he thought. An angel, in blue. Gee, he liked the way her hair fell. A woman should have long hair, he suddenly decided.

He climbed up himself and he steadied her and she let

him. First, she looked right into his eyes and then she let him. Now, they could both see over the heads of people standing around.

He felt the girl shudder. "Is it your friend?" he inquired. "Gee, I'm sorry, if it is. Can I do anything?"

"Oh, poor Pearl. Oh, Dee! Oh, Dee!" She didn't say it loud or scream or anything, but he held on to her because she might fall.

He said, "Look, if you'd want to sit down . . ." Behind them were the big soft sacks of soiled linen, filling the rear half of the truck, lying against the partition that guarded the front half where the clean stuff was carried.

She said, "Oh, Clive," faintly. She said, "I don't know what to do."

Frank told her gently that there was nothing to do but try and take it easy. The ambulance men were taking care of it. They were putting the big stout woman on the stretcher now. She was out, all right. Frank didn't think she looked dead, though. He was rather an authority.

He said, soothingly, "The lady in the black dress is going to be O.K., I should think, Ma'am. They'll take care of her, you know. Get her to the hospital, right away."

"To hospital?"

She was leaning all her weight on him, now . . . a sweet delicious burden it was. He bore it with steady strength, careful not to let his feeling intrude upon her need. "Sure," he soothed. "That's just what they'll do."

Now, the white coat working over the redhead looked up at the tallish man who was talking to the cop and mopping his face with a bloody handkerchief. There was some exchange. The man nodded. He went on talking nervously to the cop.

They began to bring the stretchers toward the ambulance.

Frank got a glimpse of the redhead's face and she was out, and a pretty face it was, too. So young and fair. He thought, Gosh, what do they have to go around smashing up women for?

The girl beside him was pretty shocked and pretty frightened, he could tell. He eased her back against the soft sacks and he said, "Aw, it's probably not too bad. I mean, gee, they can do miracles, now. I got kinda banged up last spring and you should see how the medics put me back together."

The girl looked right into his eyes again and he was almost willing to swear she'd never been down here on earth before. She said, "Did they?"

"They sure did. They're wonderful."

"Are they?" She trembled. "Was it in a hospital?"

"Sure it was." He was talking to reassure her. "I was in eight weeks. Gee, it was wonderful what they did and good food and everything."

Her neck bent as if the little head dropped under the weight of that glorious hair. "I'm not . . . feeling very well."

He said, "Gee, I'm sorry. Gee, I don't wonder." And his arm was all the way around her and she leaned on it and sank with it against the sacks . . . as if she was pretty beat. Frank didn't know exactly what he was going to do about her but he wasn't going to take his arm away. Not yet, anyhow.

The tall man and the cop moved closer to the ambulance. They were set, to Frank's sight, like a picture in the truck's door-frame. The crowd was not noisy any more but respectful toward pain and possible tragedy. So it became possible for the words between these men to be heard and understood by the young people deep inside the linen service truck.

136

The cop said, "That's O.K. then, and I got the names. Another thing, though. I understand from L.A. we are supposed to pick up this Pearl Dean. Supposed to be a Laila Breen with her. You know about that?"

The tall man, whose back was toward the truck, said stupidly. "What?"

"Same name," said the cop sharply. "You're Breen."

"Oh, my cousin, you mean." The man had a cut on his face. It was patched with adhesive but he kept mopping at it.

"Thought you said this one was your cousin."

"Yes, Miss Allison. Yes, she is my cousin."

"Look," said the cop, "you could be in shock but . . . uh . . . be obliged if you'd kinda try and explain about these cousins."

"You see, we thought Laila might be with Miss Dean. Don't you see?" said the tall man. "She's been poisoned. I guess you heard that. So naturally, we were trying to catch her." He swung his head from side to side. "But she . . . wasn't in the car, was she? Excuse me, I'm kind of mixed up myself. I mean, we thought she *was*."

The girl in the blue coat began to shudder and Frank let his arm tighten.

"I don't see her," Clive said.

"Wearing a pink suit, eh?"

"Yes, she was," Clive said.

"I don't understand," the girl was whimpering. "I don't understand."

Frank said, "Come on, lean back. Just fall back, why don't you? You mustn't worry. They're just going to the hospital."

She said faintly, "*They* are going to a hospital?"

"Sure. Sure they are."

* * *

The ambulance driver in his seat, the attendant inside. The cops sprang to clear some bystanders from its path.

"They're going right now," Frank said.

"Pearl, and Dee, are going to a hospital? Not me?"

"Sssh," said Frank, touching her hair with his free hand. "I'll find out which one for you. The cop will know. You can call up. Or you can *go* to the hospital. It'll be all right. Don't be afraid."

Her hand went out in a frightened gesture and Frank caught it in his own.

The ambulance started. It purred, it leaped, its siren began softly and swelled and then, in the distance, it fell and rose again. And it was gone.

The man with the handkerchief seemed to sigh.

Someone was shouting. "Break it up. Let the wrecker in now."

The cop said, loudly, "Wait a minute. What about the trailer?"

Clive said, spinning nervously, "Oh my God, the trailer! That's right. The trailer!" And he turned, the handkerchief half over his face.

Frank saw the cop push by and leave the pictureframe. Gently, he let the girl rest on the cushioning sacks and he, himself, came forward. He leaned to see around the open door. Mike Torres was making his way through the tangle. They were breaking up this jam, now. They'd have to be moving. He pulled his head back and looked at his blue angel. Gee, he didn't want to lose her. He didn't want to let her go. She just didn't look as if she'd have such a thing as a telephone number.

He saw that she looked like a very frightened angel, now. She was staring at something behind him. He turned his head and saw that the tall man with the bloody

138

handkerchief, from about twenty feet away, was staring in and straight at her.

Frank said, sharply, "Do you know that guy? Is he a friend of yours?"

She stiffened. She said clearly, "I know him but he tells too many lies." Her eyes lifted to Frank and Frank felt it like a blow in the heart. She said, "Would you help me?"

"*Would* I!" He turned again. The man was just staring. Frank lashed him with a look like a sword. He said, "Ma'am, do you live around here?"

"No. Oh, no."

"You don't want to get down? You don't want to be with him?"

"No. Oh, no."

"You want to go home?"

Her eyes filled. "I can never go home . . ."

Frank said, "Don't cry. How can I help you?"

"Take me to the hospital."

"I will. I will. Just lean back. And don't worry. I'll see that you're all right. Just let me shut these doors. I'll be in front, right over that wooden wall. My driver's coming. He might not let me . . . But you be quiet for a little bit until we get away from here. Then we'll call up and we'll find out and we'll go anywhere you want." She wasn't crying. She was smiling and her face was rosier. "I'd do anything to help you," said Frank and he meant every throbbing syllable.

He leaped to the ground and closed the doors. He closed her in there.

A cop said, "Get this truck outa here, will you, bud?"

"O.K. O.K."

Frank gave the motionless, staring man one more sword-sharp defiant so-what-are-you-going-to-do-about- it glare, and then he ran around the truck and got in. He reared up immediately and peered over the partition. She was snug. She was there. He hadn't lost her yet. "O.K." he whispered.

Mike came jolting down into his seat, grumbling. "Aw right, officer. I'm getting gone. Can't a man try and do a little service to his fellow citizens . . . ?"

"They get your name and address?" snapped the cop.

"Yeah. Yeah."

"O.K. then. Move."

So the linen service truck began to move along.

Clive stood in the road. He began to mop his cheek again.

Laila lay on the linen sacks. She felt comfortable, and quiet and protected. This strange young man knew about the hospital. He was taking her there. In Laila's tired and confused and too ignorant mind, there was only one hospital. She knew he wasn't afraid. She resolved she would not be afraid, either. She felt safe.

Chapter Sixteen

Vince Procter sent his cab along at a steady, skilful pace that was not spectacular but truly speedy. He said to this Talbot: "Sure. I could pick him out blindfolded. You know, I thought there was funny business, right away. So I hung around and when he comes outa the house alone, I sez to him, 'What's your angle, bud?' I sez, 'Anything in it for me?' I figure, see, if he bites on that why that gives it away. I mean, for instance, if I sez, 'Ain't she the girl that's supposed to go to the hospital?' And he sez, 'No, it ain't.' What can I do?"

"What *did* he say?" Andy's tone didn't commit him to belief in this version of Vince's behaviour.

"Said nothin'. Looked scared. Said nothin'." Vince sucked a tooth loudly. "So then I go and call in. I figure . . ."

"Wait a minute," Andy cut in. "You told him, right then and there, that the girl had been poisoned and needed treatment? You told him by what you said?"

"Why, I . . . I . . . yeah, I guess I . . . I dunno." Vince felt chagrin.

"I wish you knew," said Andy. "Because if you did and he turned right around to go back into that house, knowing something he had not known until then . . . why, we've got to give him the benefit of the doubt. He is still a liar. But he may have been trying to wiggle out of looking like a damn fool or worse. Yet, he *did* put us on her trail."

141

"I don't get it."

"Never mind. Try and remember, though. Will you? If you didn't tell him the news about Laila Breen, then he knew it before you spoke to him. Because he sure knew it, all right, three seconds after you drove away. I heard him say so."

"I don't remember exactly what I said, every word," said Vince sulkily. "I didn't take no recording."

He remembered, well enough. It made him a little uneasy, too. It didn't sound so good or so clever. Sounded entirely too much like Vince had been trying on a little blackmail. Like Vince might have been willing to throw in with that Clive or whoever he was.

He said bitterly, "What a crumb! For the money, eh? Let the little girl get so sick she'll probably die, huh?"

Andy said savagely, "If he knew she'd been poisoned when he took her there, crumb is not the word."

They sped along in silence. "Hit Lemon Grove as soon as you can," Andy told him again. "You're going to do that?"

"I am," said Vince. "Listen, I know this town."

"Lemon Grove is the only one I'm sure of. It's five o'clock. If we don't catch up with them while they are still on this Lemon Grove, we'll be sunk."

"Yeah?"

"I've lost my guide."

"Yeah?" Then Vince asked curiously, "Whadd'ya mean, guide? Who was your guide?"

"My—A red-haired girl."

"Ran out on you, did she?"

"We parted. Are we making time?"

"Good time," soothed Vince. "Say, Mr. Talbot, what's your interest in this kid? The one with the long hair. What hair, huh?"

142

"My interest?" said Andy. "To save her life."

"How come she got away in the first place?"

"She — just ran away."

"Baby stunt, eh?"

"She's rather a baby. She can't help it. She was — hurt."

"Dames," said Vince. "Young and old. All the same. They get hurt and boy, this explains *any*thing. How about the redhead? *She* run away?"

"No," said Andy. "That one never ran away in her life and never will. She guessed right, that's all. How far to Lemon Grove — "

"Not far. Not far."

"Now, tell me, you were there." Andy went back to worrying about the problem of Clive. "You heard the Fleming woman tell the police that the girl was with Pearl Dean. Did she say anything about Breen?"

"Nope. Said nothing but 'yes' when they asked her. Far as I heard. That made any sense, I mean. She was all confused. Man, she was crying and talking about 'Dearest Pearl' and universal healing or sumpin like that. She was a mess. They couldn't get no sense outa her."

He licked his lips. "You know what I'd like to see, Mr. Talbot? Huh? I'd just like to see us walk up to that crumb and say nothin'. No, I'd look at him and if it's the same one, I'd give you a nod or sumpin and you sock him. This I'd like to see."

"I'd like to sock him," admitted Andy.

"This I'd like. Just the two of us walk up, and whammy, he's cold." Vince was dreaming a pleasant dream. He liked the drama of it. He liked the consequences. This cousin or whatever he was, out cold. And speechless. Vince thought it would save a lot of argument if this Clive got speechless pretty fast. It was just a dream.

Andy Talbot wasn't dreaming. He was feeling a cold

rage, but all his training and conviction were telling him to make sure it rested on a fact. So he said, "Go over that conversation for me."

"What conversation?"

"You and Breen."

"I told you the gist of it," Vince said shortly.

"We'll know something," said Andy out of his own thought stream, "if and when we catch up with Pearl Dean. If Clive has caught her in good faith, that will be that."

"Yeah," said Vince gloomily.

"But if he has not, if he's got Dee held up somewhere instead . . ." Then Andy grinned, "Although I don't think it'll be easy to hold up Dee Allison."

"That the redhead?" said Vince.

"Red as they come."

"Your girl friend, Mr. Talbot?"

"She's a friend," said Andy rather bitterly.

"You're partial to the little one with the black hair?" Vince couldn't *get* this boy and girl stuff.

"Call me just a friend to both of them," snapped Andy, "but if she dies, I'm nobody's friend."

Vince swallowed. "I sure hope I can do something to help this work out all right," he said. "Sure like to see him get his, that crumb."

Talbot said harshly, "Don't worry. If I get convinced Breen's been trying to let the girl stay lost, I'll let him have it."

"Yeah," said Vince, brightening.

Old Mrs. Gilman leaned so far out of her chair that she nearly tipped over. She could see and she could hear and she could understand but she could not speak. And sometimes her mind went frantic. She had to use all the control she could muster to keep from fainting in despair. For, because she could not speak, people assumed she was no longer intelligent. People spoke to her in simple words, slowly and loudly. People spoke before her as if she were not there, or as if she were a child and could not understand swift sentences with polysyllabic words in them. No one expected her to bear witness and now, when she was an intelligent and competent witness, she was not asked.

The policeman was looking for the girl with the long black hair. He had searched the trailer and found it empty. The man with adhesive on his face was tearing his hair about it. The girl, he said, was in danger and must be found. He was making a frantic fuss.

So now they were asking questions, asking the neighbours who knew nothing. Asking Agnes Nilsson, who stood and answered with the nothing that she knew. And would not heed Mrs. Gilman's tapping fingers at all.

It was deliberate. Mrs. Gilman knew this. The signal was well understood between them. It meant, "Give me pencil and paper. I have something to communicate." Mrs. Gilman could not walk into the house to get pencil and paper for herself. Nor could she lift her chair over the eight-inch threshold. But no one but Agnes knew this signal.

The policeman had said, "What's wrong with the lady? Can't talk, can she?"

And Agnes, just as if Mrs. Gilman were incompetent to understand, had shaken her head and said in a low voice, "She's a little unstable emotionally since her accident."

Mrs. Gilman had seen the policeman nod sagely and seen his eyes evade her own with the distaste of the normal for that which is not. She vowed again in her soul to get rid

145

of Agnes Nilsson. Next time her sons came, she would insist. She would write it and write it, until they took heed. She would make them listen. She still thought. Listen.

But she knew Agnes would only purr the long words that Agnes loved. The words that people respected, not for their sense but their implication of wisdom. Lies. Lies in polysyllables. If Agnes had said "She is crazy," they would soon resent it. Agnes was too smart for that.

Oh how Mrs. Gilman wanted paper and pencil to tell the policeman, and the poor chap who was so anxious, exactly where the girl was now. She had seen. She had understood. She could read. She knew the name of the firm painted on the side of that truck. Paramount Linen Service. She even knew the licence number. Her memory was firm. Her mind was clear. She could tell them where the girl had gone.

Agnes was saying, "I don't think there was any such girl as you describe. Of course, I left this porch. I am *not* an R.N." Agnes always said this in such a huff that it seemed to be someone else's fault, not hers. "But I've had so much experience, I felt I might be useful . . ."

"You went the other side of the trailer, then? Maybe the old lady . . . You don't think . . . ? Can she talk on her fingers?"

"A little," said Agnes condescendingly. "She craves attention, you see." Mrs. Gilman could hear that soft sly statement. Then Agnes with her face hardening spoke more loudly, "I should not have left her. After all, *she* is my charge." Agnes looked locked to her duty.

But Mrs. Gilman sighed and fell back. So, Agnes felt guilty. No use, then. When Agnes felt guilty, there was only one person she could take it out on.

Mrs. Gilman's tired eyelids fell. They'd have to find out

146

where the girl had gone, in some other way.

The truck marked Paramount Linen Service scooted north and then west. Mike Torres was lecturing on the subject of authority. Once you gave a man a uniform and a little authority, Mike proclaimed, he is not the same man as he was. Frank Turner appeared to be listening with grave respect. But he was wondering just how he was going to get the girl in the blue coat to the hospital, as he had promised. He didn't know yet the name of that friend she wanted to see. And he didn't know which hospital it was, where that friend had been taken. He was pretty sure the truck was going farther and farther away from whichever hospital it was.

There came a moment when Mike stopped talking. Then Frank asked him whether he knew.

"Where they took them? Sure. St. Bart's. Long Beach, I guess. Why? Whadd'ya want to know for?"

Frank hesitated. It was a good chance to tell. All he had to do was answer the question. If he did, he guessed Mike would dump him and the girl, right then and there. He'd be out of a job, and that didn't bother him so much, but he kept remembering that he didn't have but about four bucks in his pocket.

"You got a look at that redhead, I bet," Mike chuckled, answering his own question. "Listen, kid. She was a stunner, all right, but it don't pay to get romantic ideas about a perfect stranger. For all you know, she's married and got eight red-headed kids. Hey?"

"Was she hurt much?" Frank asked. He thought perhaps the red-headed girl was his angel's friend, for whom she was so afraid.

"I doubt it," Mike said. "She musta seen it coming, and

147

she knew how to get limp and protect herself. She was out, all right, but she didn't get no bones broken. They didn't *think*. Of course," Mike's habitual gloom reasserted itself, "there could be something internal. You never know, you know." Mike brooded. "For natural causes," proclaimed Mike suddenly, "I'm going to stop here a minute."

As soon as the door marked *Men* had closed on Mike, Frank was up and back in the truck's clean-linen compartment, looking over the partition. He was going to suggest, if she didn't mind, that they might wait until they were near a bus line before they told Mike and got thrown out. He was going to ask if she was in any special hurry. Or if she wanted to tell him her friend's name, so he could jump out now and call St. Bart's on the phone and inquire. Then, maybe there'd be someplace else he could take her, and wait until visiting hours.

But he didn't ask any of these questions.

She was asleep. She was just curled quietly back there, sound asleep. She must be awful tired and beat, and sleep was a healing thing. . . . Asleep! Ah, let her sleep! Maybe he could work it so Mike wouldn't know. He thought of a way. He'd tell Mike he'd take the truck in alone. It was so late. When they went past Mike's corner right half a block from where Mike's supper was waiting, all Frank had to do was suggest this. Mike would be tempted.

Then, the girl could sleep on. Then, he could even take off, truck and all, and take her home. She'd said she could never go home. But Frank could. He had one. His heart kind of caught in his throat when he thought of it. Suppose she didn't have any place to go for the night, for instance. He could take her home with him, then. Ma wouldn't mind. Ma would see it the way Frank saw it. Frank considered his mother a rattle-brained female, for

148

which he kidded and adored her. Ma wouldn't even ask any questions except if the girl was hungry. Ma never suspected anybody of being anything but a human being, which was reckless and rattle-brained. But swell.

Ma wouldn't mind. He'd lift her gently to the bed in the front room. She'd never wake, so gentle he could be.

When Mike came back he looked hard at the lad's face, grunted, got in, snapped his headlights on. The truck started. "What's with you?" asked Mike suddenly.

"Hm?"

"You got the funniest look on your puss."

"Have I? Gee, I . . . I dunno . . ."

"Nothing to sit there *smiling* about, that I can see. We're going to be late as hell pulling in and the boss won't want to believe . . ."

Frank kept his face stiff and appeared to be listening.

When Dee Allison opened her eyes she thought for a moment she was in the hospital. The white coat on the attendant was the first thing she recognized. But then, as her senses recovered their touch on the rest of the environment, she knew she was in an ambulance.

She promptly sat up.

Just as promptly, the attendant pushed her down. "Now," he soothed, "you're O.K., Miss Allison. Nothing much wrong with you at all. Now, we'll take care of you." He had a smooth young face.

Dee lay and looked at him, waiting for all her wits and a full memory to return. She thought she had better be careful. This was no time to start blazing. It was almost as if Andy Talbot said in her ear, "Use your head, Dee." Yes, she had better be smart and avoid, if she could, showing any misery that would tempt this lad to put her out of it.

Dee thought that she might be drugged, fast, if she showed cause.

Finally she asked, quietly, "Did they find Laila Breen?"

"Now . . ."

"You haven't heard that name? She wasn't in the trailer?" Dee was being so cool and calm, he had to answer.

He said soothingly, "I believe there *was* a *Mr.* Breen."

"Yes. What happened to him?"

"He's all right. He wasn't hurt."

"I see," she said. She had a brief recollection of a very brief and unbelievable impression. It had seemed to her, for one second, that Clive had *meant* to smash into something. She couldn't be thinking quite straight. Her head felt swollen.

She said, "I suppose the police were there?"

"Oh yes. They were there."

Dee let herself feel relieved. Surely, surely, Laila was found and all was well. Unless . . . She said, "Was there another girl injured?"

"Just this lady."

Dee turned her head and saw the big bare forehead, the lank hair, the sagging mouth, the unconsciousness of Pearl Dean. Her heart leaped in sorrow and alarm. "How *is* Miss Dean?" she asked, keeping her voice hushed and steady.

"Ribs," he told her. "Thigh fracture. Maybe more. You know her?"

Dee said, "Yes, I do. Was the trailer hit?"

"What trailer is that, Miss Allison?"

Dee bit her lips sharply. She said carefully, "I am trying to find out what happened to a girl named Laila Breen. I believe she was riding in a trailer behind Miss Dean's coupé."

150

He looked just blank.

"Was there any other ambulance there?"

"No, Miss Allison."

"Then if she was there she is still there." Dee lost her control a little. "But *she* ought to be going to a hospital! Why didn't Clive send her with us?" Her voice was rising. "*I'm* all right. You shouldn't have *me*. You've got the wrong girl! Where's Laila?"

Pearl Dean's deep voice came booming, "Doctor," it said. "Laila. Poison. Doctor."

As the attendant bent over her, Pearl's eyelids rolled up and the huge eyes were revealed, full of fear and pain. He said, "Now, Miss Dean . . ."

Dee thought she saw his intention. She thought he was going to put this one out of her misery, right away. She cried, "Pearl! It's Dee. Quick, tell me. Where is Laila?"

"Laila's in the trailer," said Pearl. Her words came faster. "Clive Breen put her in the trailer."

"Oh, Pearl . . . ! You and Clive . . . !"

"Not I. Not I. No one told me. I heard the voice. I turned to go back. To the doctor. I am not such a *fool,* Dee." Pearl tried to raise herself. "What was the poison? I didn't make the turn! I didn't make it! Where is Laila? Where is she now?" The big woman had lost all her calm and her majesty. She was shrill and frantic for her child.

Dee said, "Oh, Pearl! Too bad. She must be . . . back there. Laila must be with Clive."

The woman's eyes rolled. Pain caught up with her. She had one more sentence, and it came in her old pompous boom and dignity. "Clive is not good for her," said Pearl Dean.

The siren wailed. The attendant was bending over Pearl, who seemed to have fainted. Dee gathered the muscles of her legs like springs. "I've got to get out of here," said Dee to herself. So she sat up, stealthily, behind the attendant's back.

He knew it, though. He turned around quickly.

She said, quietly, steadily, "A girl is going to die if I don't get back there. Another girl. Not I."

He said, just as quietly, "When we get to the hospital, you can tell someone. We're going to Long Beach. We are nearly there."

Dee said, "Don't drug me, please. This is very important."

He was not qualified to give her a hypo but cautiously he did not say so. "Will you lie back, then? I have to do my job, Miss Allison."

So Dee lay back. "I understand," she said, still speaking quietly. "I don't think you believe me, do you? Yet that girl's situation is being broadcast, all over the city."

"By the police?"

"Yes, I . . ."

"Nothing to worry about, then."

Dee said, "It's a little different than they know. Somebody doesn't *want* her found and saved."

The attendant raised his eyebrows, amiably enough. But his mind was on his own responsibility.

So Dee was quiet.

Chapter Seventeen

By five-forty, the mess at the crossroads was yielding to order. Some people still stood about in knots, still talking it over, but many had gone on about their business already. All the undamaged vehicles had pulled away, leaving the intersection to the wreckers, working to tear apart and tow away Pearl's coupé, and Andy's convertible, to haul off the Buick with the bashed bonnet. The trailer, on the margin of the road, remained where it had come to rest, since it was not an obstacle to traffic.

The red panel truck still stood with its nose in the road. Traffic, however, was still blocked off. In front of the TV remote truck, drawn up on the Baxter property, there was an argument going on. Meantime, some of the TV people were frantically busy. But some were self-importantly defending themselves to the policeman, who seemed annoyed and took no interest in the driving necessities of their time-ridden profession.

Clive Breen, still making play with the handkerchief in a nervous repetition, leaned on a mailbox near the trailer. He felt very shaky. He was trying to think what he would do now, if he were as innocent as he wished to appear. He was trying to think, at the same time, about the truth, and so his mind whirled in two ways at once. Clive got hold of himself enough to take one thing at a time.

Truly, Laila was gone. She would not be found *here*. What would become of her, now, rested on pure chance.

There was nothing Clive could do about it. Even had he wanted to, he could not have told what kind of truck it was in which she had been carried away. No, she was gone, afloat on the mercy of that kid who had shut those doors. He, Clive, had *not* seen her. Clive would never admit that he had been *able* to see her. All right, maybe he had known she was in the trailer, but now she had disappeared!

He was getting mixed up again, between the true and the false. Wait a minute.

If Laila were found soon enough, he could be ruined and undone. But she was lost. And if she were lost long enough, he thought he could probably squirm out of it. A chance, still . . .

Pearl Dean and Dee, hauled off to a hospital, were *hors de combat. They* wouldn't be looking for Laila for a while. Pearl Dean, he felt sure, would not live — not long. They would keep Dee; Dee was no factor. The police had no idea where to look, and Laila was hidden, and time kept passing. It was getting toward six o'clock. Getting dark. Incongruously, in the warm September weather, the sun still followed the year's pattern and it was going down.

Clive pondered. If he were innocent, what would he do? Phone Dr. Stirling, he thought. Yes, he'd better. But he hung back. He was in shock from the accident, or so he could say. He could take a little more time to pull himself together.

He had not exactly meant to hit the coupé. And yet, he had meant to do some smashing thing. Pearl's passing the man with the flag was a kind of opportunity. He hadn't wanted to hurt Pearl Dean. But in some ways it was better than if he'd hit that trailer. He shook.

He thought a good lawyer could get him out of this accident mess. There were so many other people involved — he wasn't worried. But he saw, now, that he had time to

154

think a minute if he, Clive, her heir, had accidentally — well, say — injured Laila. That wouldn't have been so good.

One thing, surely nobody had ever been through so nerve-wracking a series of experiences as he, in the last hours. In a way, it was a pity he could never make a yarn of it. How many hairbreadths had he been from exposure, how many times? But, by a combination of good luck and quick thinking and he knew not what else, here he was, and there was still a chance . . . he kept thinking it a better and better chance . . . that everything was going to turn out all right for Clive. If he could only remember the truth from the lies.

Clive began to feel stronger. Phone? He glanced up toward the porch of the house. In the dusk he could distinguish a woman in a wheel-chair, a nurse in a grey uniform, and a woman in a print dress. He didn't feel like encountering them. He didn't want chatter.

He glanced at the house across the road. Before this one swarmed that knot of men. And all those cars. The TV truck, that red truck, and two passenger cars . . . all parked carelessly, making a kind of wall. And in the road there was an argument. But the house was dark and silent, obviously vacant or in the process of being vacated. The door on this side of the house was wide open. Clive concluded that there would be no phone connected in there.

So it would have to be the gas station or the little store. He chose the gas station which was catty-corner, as most likely to have a closed booth. Now, he must choose and cross two sides of the square.

He chose to cross toward the arguing men. They were too busy to pay him any attention. He could hear scraps of the argument, the loud voices lapping each other.

"For your information, we got to set up here . . ."

"I don't care . . ."

"And that takes time. . . . We're late. We go on the air at *seven!*"

"You see those wrecks, don't you?"

"Little matter of a sponsor's money and what he's got a right to expect . . ."

"Don't care *who* you know . . ."

"We had a right to place that truck in our picture. And our man had a flag—"

"I want names, addresses and some cooperation—"

"We're busy! We're busy! You don't understand our problem."

"Public safety is my . . ."

"Our job to do, too."

Clive started to leave this south-west corner, to skirt the red truck, and take a curving course around the wreckers struggling in the centre of the roads. But as he reached a point where he could see down the road to the west, what he saw turned him and sent him scuttling to the shelter of that red truck, where he stood jittering and undone.

Two men were walking fast in the deserted roadway, coming here. One of the men was Andrew Talbot, and that was not so startling. But the other man was the cab-driver! The same one. The one who would know Clive Breen at sight. The one whom he had thought never to see again.

Clive didn't have *this* thought though.

He didn't know what he must say, exactly.

He realised that he could not run up any empty road and get away. It was not yet dark enough for that. Nor were there any trees, no thicket here in which to hide himself. No hedge. Yes, there was a hedge — a thick-clipped line of pittosporum, about four feet high, along the walk to the side door of this vacant house. It divided the neat front-yard from the less formal back-yard of the corner plot. Clive realised that no one in the wrangling group the other side of this truck could see him, now. And if he slipped back, beyond the red truck, and reached the hedge, the people catty-cornered could not see him, either, from where they stood before the store.

No one could see him but those women on that porch, and if he were to slip to the other side of the hedge and into the side door of this vacant house, there he could lie low. He must! He must! His nerves would not hold.

The women on the porch were not looking this way. The nurse had her back to him and she blocked the vision of the one in the print dress. The old lady in the chair was lying back as if she were tired or maybe even asleep. Old and invalid as she was, probably half-blind in this poor light, what did it matter if she did see?

He must! Must hide! There was nothing else that he could bear to do.

So he did it. Trucks and cars, parked like spokes of a fan, shielded him from a casual glance, as he went, fast and slippery, and hidden behind the house corner, he slipped inside. It was ten minutes to six and the light was leaving the sky.

Agnes Nilsson, big, strong, blonde, hard-eyed, soft-voiced, gripped the handles of the wheel-chair. "Excuse us, Miz Johannes. Mrs. Gilman must go indoors and rest now."

"Not going to watch the TV, Mrs. Gilman?" the neighbour asked. Mrs. Gilman nodded.

But Agnes said, "Oh, not now. She *had* planned . . . But not after all this excitement. Much too much for her."

Mrs. Gilman's fingers drummed.

"She can watch it on her screen, indoors," said Agnes soothingly, "while she has her nice supper. Just as she does every Wednesday."

"My husband's so crazy about *It's a Living*," said Mrs. Johannes. "Of course, I'm not. I get a little bored with that programme. Always the *same*, it seems to me. Of course, it is different when they *do* the show right here in the neighbourhood. I don't want to miss *that*."

I don't want to miss it, either, wailed Mrs. Gilman silently in her scarred and broken throat. Oh, I don't. She tried to brake the chair's wheels with her thin hands.

But Agnes, pretending not to notice, tipped the chair, and the wheels went over the threshold. Agnes pushed her inside. The dead familiar closed around her. All the lovely excitement was shut away. It was not for Mrs. Gilman to be altogether alive, any more.

The moment the ambulance came to a stop, Dee Allison, coiled in a tension she hoped did not show, was ready and watching for her chance.

Every red hair on her head was determined. For herself and her own state of health, she had no concern. She felt battered but well enough and she was not going to be on the sidelines. She knew better than to get herself entrapped in hospital regulations, where they would preach incapacity, where they believed in it. Until Laila was found and safe, Dee Allison wasn't going to be incapacitated or made to concede that she was.

She knew where the ambulance had brought her. This was Long Beach. She had watched as many turns as she could. She knew exactly what she was going to do. If a chance came, she was going to get away.

They handled Pearl first and it was Pearl who produced the chance. The stretcher was tilting, half in, half out, when Pearl suddenly came to life. Pearl's head raised. Pearl's fat arms went back of her head, with what pain only Pearl knew, and Pearl's hands were scrabbling, scratching and grabbing for the white coat carrying her head, and Pearl's voice boomed . . . "Now, Dee! Now! Go to Laila!" And Dee, with amazement exploding in her mind, was still ready.

So she flashed through, under, and around the men and the stretcher on which Pearl was writhing, and then Dee was running as fast as her pretty legs would carry her, with shouts in the gathering dusk behind her.

But they could not drop poor Pearl, their hands were full of Pearl. She thought she heard someone running, a female calling, but nobody caught her. Dee was around the corner of the hospital grounds and into a shopping street, through the doors of a dime store and out again at the side. . . . The store was closing. Luck, she thought. No one could follow, now. She drew up gasping on the sidewalk.

In all this swift activity of legs and breath, Dee's mind remained amazed. Pearl had read her tension and her mind. There was such a thing as telepathy, then. Or intuition. Or something not always in the list we count on. Pearl had tried to help. Pearl, too, was thinking of Laila Breen and *her* peril, with no more regard for Pearl's pain than Dee had for her own. Dee felt like weeping, for just a moment. She hoped . . . she hoped the big woman would be healed of her injuries. She felt a double burden, now. Her own anxiety for Laila was the heavier for Pearl Dean's.

No time to be amazed. Making her mood brisk, Dee looked about her. Long Beach. She stood gasping on the sidewalk and home-going people jostled her. Dee had no purse any more, and no money. But she could telephone. Somebody would give her a coin or two.

Sublimely sure of it, Dee stopped a bent and hurrying woman in a shabby grey coat. "I've lost my purse," she said breathlessly. "Could you please loan me some dimes to phone my friends?"

The woman straightened from her driving walk. Silently, she opened her purse and handed Dee some silver.

"Thank you. Thank you. Thank you."

The woman smiled. "I was pretty when I was younger. You want to be more careful."

"Yes, I . . . will." Dee's eyes widened.

"But I know how it is. I . . . remember." The woman nodded and scurried on her way.

Amazed, and cancelling amazement, Dee ran into a drugstore. All her instincts said hurry. Go back there. She dialled Stirling's number and it was busy. Wild with impatience, she dialled Jonas's house.

"Lorraine?"

"Oh yes. Miss Dee!"

"Listen. You call Dr. Stirling. I can't get him. Tell him this. Write it down. *There was an accident but I'm all right.* Tell him that. *Laila was in Pearl's trailer. Clive put her there and Pearl told me so.* Got it, Lorraine? *Now, I am going back to the corner of Lemon Grove and Neptune Road. The trailer is there.* That'll do, I think. He'll understand."

"Miss Dee, did you find her?"

"I know where she *was,*" Dee told her. "Call him as soon as you can, Lorraine. Good-bye."

Now, to get back. It would be east and north of here. Not far. Dee still had no money but that didn't worry her.

Nothing easier than to hitch a ride. In the rumpled green with her flaming hair, her fabulous colouring, she was conspicuous, and she was vivid and determined, and she got a ride.

The man who picked her up may have had wolfish intentions but if so they were frustrated. For Dee, with the sure skill that she'd begun to learn with her first lipstick, took him ruthlessly out of his way and into hers. And when they ran into a road block, she abandoned him, giving sweet thanks and no mercy. He was left, gnawing his lip, a good Samaritan whether he would or no.

It was getting dark. Dee's head pained her, now and then. Sometimes she was a little dizzy. But she ran in a weary shuffle north along the car-less road. The next crossroad could not be far and it would be the scene of the accident. Police would be there and maybe Laila found, and all well. If not, she could explain, and get after Clive and Laila quickly.

It must be nearly six o'clock. Less than six hours to find Laila now. They couldn't be sure of more margin than that. Stop thinking about time. Use it. Keep going. Dee put her head down and slogged along. A tentacle touched her heart as she wondered if poor Mrs. Vaughn would live.

She thought, Laila . . . was my job. I should have kept her out of danger. Pearl could see the danger but I could not and I wasn't good at the job. Now I must do every last ounce of trying that I can to find her or I can't stand it. I couldn't live any more.

She kept going. She didn't in her conscious thoughts hold Andrew Talbot, but every throb of her labouring heart beat in a hollow where his name had been.

Chapter Eighteen

In the half dark, Talbot walked into the snarl of men and up to the cop and said tensely, "What happened here? That's my car. Where's Dee Allison?"

The snarl broke apart. The argument, about to die of its own futility, ceased. The civilians dashed to their business at once. Some of them joined the TV technicians who were rolling out equipment in furious haste and lost themselves in that systematic disorder. Two workmen and a Mr. Bowman gathered together, out of their way. Mr. Bowman, who was dressed as elegantly as he would be in his life, took paper from his pocket. It was too dark to read but he began to mumble half-memorised phrases, anyway. His eyes were faintly glazed. A man approached him, turned him round, and began to smear make-up on his face.

The cop said, "Is your name Talbot?"

"Where's Dee Allison?" Talbot was wild with alarm. Vince Procter shifted his weight from foot to foot beside him, peering at everything, enjoying the excited confusion.

"Allison? That's the red-headed girl? Yeah, well, she got hurt some. Not bad. Ambulance took her to St. Bart's. That's this end of Long Beach."

"Not bad? *How* bad?"

"Knocked her out, but nothing broken. Nothing serious, as far as I know."

"Where's Breen? He was in my car, too."

"Oh, he's around. Or he was. He's O.K." The cop looked glad to be giving good news.

Andy pulled air into his lungs. "That coupé belongs to Pearl Dean?"

"Woman in the coupé? Yeah, she was injured all right. She was the worst. Ambulance took her, too. Gustavson went with a friend."

"Who's he?"

"Fellow in the Buick. He was just groggy. Lucky, believe me."

Andy's eyes swept the crossroads which were blurring fast, through the swift twilight to true nightfall. He crossed out his impulse to go running to Dee in the hospital. She wouldn't want him there. She wouldn't need him. She was in trained hands. Now, he must find Laila for both of them. "Where's Laila Breen?" he demanded.

"That we don't know," the cop said, settling into the ground as if he dug his heels in to talk. "Listen, what do you know about that deal?"

"She was in the trailer."

"No, she wasn't, Mr. Talbot."

"She must have been."

"She wasn't there."

"Trailer smashed any?" Now Andy could see its aluminium glimmer across the way.

"Not a bit," the cop said. "Don't look it."

"Could have gotten out, then?"

"Here, you mean? Could have, but nobody saw her."

"Go on," said Andy tensely. "That's impossible."

"Well," the cop said, faintly offended. He didn't deal in impossibilities. "If you see her, you tell us. We didn't see her."

"*Nobody* saw her?"

163

"Looks to us like she never was in there. Not when it crashed."

Andy's jaw cracked. "That's possible," he admitted grudgingly. "Did you ask Pearl Dean what she'd done with her?"

"Miss Dean wasn't talking. Miss Dean was pretty unconscious, you know."

"What about Breen? Where *is* Breen?"

"Breen? He was with us when we searched the trailer. Got pretty upset. Yeah, he was around. Maybe he went in someplace, to phone or something. Probably the store."

"You're not letting traffic through here?"

"Not yet."

Andy turned his head to search the darkening crossroads again for Clive, for Laila, for a clue. The wrecker was carrying off his blue convertible but he made no move to check on where it was going or what damage had been done. He said, frowning, "Then, where could she go?"

"Laila Breen, eh? Well, maybe if you get in touch with the hospital that Miss Dean could tell you what the score is. Although, I dunno. . . ." The cop was shaking his head dolefully.

Andy swallowed. "You're sure Miss Allison wasn't badly hurt?"

"So they said. She was knocked out. I guess that's about all."

A little man wearing a stained and misshapen felt hat moved chattily in. "What happened was, this coupé . . ."

"Did you see it happen?" Andy bent a sharp look upon him.

"No, but I heard it. Man! I was working right there in that house. Me and Al, that's my partner, we ran out right away. We —"

164

"Excuse me," said Andy. He began to walk across the trafficless intersection and Vince followed at his heels.

"Watcha going to do, now, Mr. Talbot?"

"Take a look at the trailer. Find someone who saw something. Find Breen." Andy began to run. He hurried around the trailer, yanked on the sagging door, and vanished.

Vince, lingering, looked behind him. Must have been a pretty fine mess, he thought, but it was all over now. The usual miracle was happening. Another ten minutes, you'd ride by, you'd see nothing. You'd never know. Vince mused on the miracle a moment. Then he recalled himself to the business at hand and followed, around the trailer.

The cop frowned around. He advanced on the civilians. "Get these cars all the way off the road, you people. I don't care whose they are. And get this truck out of the intersection. Will it move? Who's the driver?" He put his hands on his hips. "Who's responsible?"

Mr. Bowman said stiffly, "I own that truck."

"It's got to be moved."

"It'll be moved. Right away. That's what we're *trying* to do. It's going to be televised. We're going to put it right up against the house, see . . ."

"Then, put it. I don't want no more talk, here."

"Coolie," called Bowman. "Come here."

The little man in the old felt hat came closer.

"Listen, ask the TV people, see if it's all right to move the truck in, now. And then I want you and Al to make the check and stand by."

"Sure, boss. Hey, Al . . ."

The bigger workman got into the truck. "How do you

165

want it?"

Bowman, transfixed, was looking at the little man. "Coolie, you'll have to take off that hat."

"What hat? This hat?"

The policeman snapped. "How about the truck?"

Coolie ducked away and accosted one of the TV men. Bowman looked harassed. There ensued a loud discussion about moving the truck. And the dark came down.

Dee's feet, bruised through her soft slippers, were heavy and sore. Cars were coming up behind her, now, their headlights and shadows dizzied her sight. She felt confused. She could see the street light and the traffic light ahead. She came stumbling slowly northward up the left side of the road.

Traffic was moving. There seemed to be no sign of any accident. The whole scene was unfamiliar. She could not get her bearings. She stopped her weary slogging to look about her and consider. Just around the corner on the road's shoulder some cars were bucking and backing.

Then she saw in the vague light that was shed down only upon crossroads, a gleam of aluminium, ahead of her and across the road. She would have begun to run toward the corner toward the place where she could cross with the light and get to the trailer herself, but there was a strangled sound somewhere near her in the dark. She looked and she thought she must have gone mad! Something must press upon and confuse her brain! Her cousin Clive was half-crouching against a hedge.

She was so close upon him that she could see his grey suit, his collar, and the startled roll of the eye in the pale oval of his face, and the weapon, which was the mad thing, a long gun, perhaps a rifle, that rested across his white hands.

There were alternatives for Dee. She could scream. She could run. She could go on thinking she'd gone mad.

She chose none of these. If she was not mad, then he was there. The long gun's snout was tending toward the trailer across the road.

She said clearly, in a cousinly voice, "What are you doing, Clive? *Is* it Clive? I can barely see —"

But she could see. That his hands and arms moved nervously and secretively to thrust the gun into the thick shrub beside which he was standing. He turned his body and wavered like a shadow.

"Where's Laila?" Dee said calmly. "I've come back for her."

"In there," Clive said. She followed the shift of his head. "She's asking for you," said Clive. "She wants you, Dee. It's lucky you came."

Dee saw the open door at the side of this house on the corner. She was convinced in one sudden surge of her imagination that Laila was somehow hurt and in that house. The scene was vivid to her, as if she were already *there* and could see Laila lying still with her black hair spreading, her eyes a little frightened. Clive had her elbow and Dee flew across fifteen feet of dark grass. The inside of the house was pitch dark. She could see nothing.

He filled the doorway behind her. He grasped her.

"Laila?" she gasped.

He grasped her fiercely. "How did you get here?" he cried into her ear.

"Where is she? Where's Laila?"

"I don't know, Dee."

"You *do* know," she flamed. "Pearl told me."

So he grasped her at her throat. "Then shut up," he said. "Shut up and get in here."

She struggled, but he had her.

Crises were a dime a dozen to Clive Breen. Damn Dee. He'd had it all so clear. He'd found the rifle by the light of a match in a kind of lumber-room in this house. Shells, too, all handy. It had seemed an omen. A hint. It was an idea. He'd been thinking it all out — watching quietly in the dark of the hedge.

Pearl Dean, who knew about him, was dying. Estelle, who knew about him, he could manage somehow. Laila, who knew about him, *must* die. The only one who knew and was hale, whole, free, and shrewd and dangerous and *here,* was the cab-driver.

Maybe he'd have shot that cab-driver. Maybe he wouldn't have had enough nerve. Or decided it wasn't wise. He'd felt calm and collected waiting there, examining the disadvantages either way. But now came Dee muddling him, getting him mixed up again between the true and false.

He was not sure that she had seen the gun. If she had he didn't know what he'd do. If she had not, he'd talk himself out. He'd talk her into being on his side. If he could talk *her* into being on his side, it wouldn't be so bad. It was like a light, a real hope. It was really a better idea than the gun and he preferred it. The trouble was, unfairly, outrageously, if she'd seen the gun, she'd probably be against him. And he didn't know, he couldn't tell.

He kept whispering, "Dee, you've got to understand. I won't let you go until you listen to me. You've got to listen. I never meant to do anything wrong. You're going to believe me. I'll make you believe me. I'm not going to let you go until you say you understand."

Dee thought, Why, he's frantic! Her head hurt. His hands hurt her. She thought, Andy was right. Clive's thought about the money from the *beginning.* Why didn't I see that Andy was right? She thought, with a feeling of

168

wild satisfaction, Well, he didn't shoot anybody. And he hasn't got Laila!

Outside, all was haste and apparent confusion. Cars bucked and roared. The red truck was shifting position. Men were shouting. Nevertheless, in someone's plan there was order and in the next orderly step, a signal was given. Out of the dim scene at the crossroads, the Baxter house sprang up. Glowing, all bathed in the converging shafts from a battery of lights, it floated out of the darkness, sharp and crisp, every nail in the boards and tarpaper over the windows was caught and seen.

The fierce light cast a sharp shadow past the open side door, but Dee could see, in some reflection, that they were struggling in a forlorn-looking kitchen. The door through which she had entered this house was the back door. Clive drew her through a doorless pantry. But light poured on the house and pierced and penetrated the very walls. She could see his sweating face and starting eyeballs. It crossed her mind at last. Clive didn't have Laila, but in some madness, he had *her*. She couldn't get away from him. She was Clive's prisoner.

And he was imprisoned by the light. Not a mouse could move through that door any more, and be unseen.

Near it, now, a man was shouting: "Get a better light around this way, you guys. Got to catch them working on this door."

"What about the front door, Mel? You want a shot inside?"

"See if you can set up for it. We can't, we can't. Can, we're going to do it."

"What's the time now?"

"Get the lead out, Gil."

"We start shooting on the truck, Mr. Bowman. After the commercial, we get the back door and then . . ."

169

"I ain't going in there with no camera, bub. You might as well . . ."

"Frame it *in* the door. Listen, I want to . . ."

"More light on the doors."

"Listen, you guys, it's after six already."

All the while, Clive fled from the light. He dragged Dee with him, hunting darkness. But the little house was wide open. Across the front, inside, living-room and dining-room partitions were mere indications. The bedroom on the inside back corner was vulnerable, too. All the interior doors were braced open. Now light attacked from the front and side. Clive nuzzled the bedroom windows but they were barricaded somehow. No way existed to the outer darkness, except through the light that poured upon the little house from two sides. Bathroom door, closet doors, were all braced open. There was one door, only one, that was not open. He had found that door before. Toward that, desperately, he dragged her.

He shoved her against it. It did not yield. So he got his arm around her neck with her throat pinched in the crook of his elbow. He turned the doorknob with his free hand, yanked, shoved her inside, and as they both tottered, he pulled the door inward. He fumbled around the lock. He knew the type. He pushed the button set in the door's edge. Now it would lock. He shut the door with a sharp click and then they fell.

They were in a small lumber room, utility room, the Californian equivalent of a cellar. There was the upright cylinder of a water-heater. Even in this place, the merciless light sprang through every crack and chink along the window. So Dee could see some rusty tools, an old ironing-board, two guns hung high on the wall, a short heavy

170

step-ladder standing at an angle, old crates and boxes of junk in the corner. Rolls of soft builder's paper lay parallel upon the floor. They had stumbled upon the unexpected step-up that these rolls of paper made.

And even as they found this refuge, and as they fell, Clive, still holding her throat in the sharp pressure of his bent arm, was still whispering fiercely, "You got to believe me, Dee. Say you believe me and I'll be glad to let you go."

But she couldn't say anything. She couldn't make a sound.

Chapter Nineteen

Talbot came in long strides across the road again.

Traffic was flowing as if the accident had never been. Bystanders were gathered now, for a different sensation. Every idle eye, magnetised by the light, was fixed on the Baxter house and the men and the microphones and the cameras around it.

Andy accosted the lookers-on with questions, but they were not willing to be too long distracted from this present enchantment. Many had not seen the accident at all. No one had seen any long-haired girl in a coral-coloured suit. No one knew where a tallish dark man in grey could have gone, although some had seen him. Some had seen the red-head. Some remembered the big woman in black. Some could tell him what he already knew.

He found a vague little man who said he thought he had seen such a girl, yes. There was something in the back of his mind. It was mixed up with the idea of height, something high . . . he couldn't just place his impression. Andy gave him up.

Meanwhile, Vince was asking at the gas station. They met on that corner. "Nothing doing," Vince said. "Those guys couldn't see a thing around the trailer."

So they ran together toward the store. It was closing. The proprietor was in a hurry to get over there and watch the programme that was going to be telecast from the Baxter house. Talbot blocked his way with questions. "Long dark hair, down her back. Pink suit."

"Hey, wait a minute Mr. Talbot." Vince was plucking his sleeve.

Andy looked at his twitching face. "What's the matter?"

"She was wearing a coat, a blue coat. I thought I told you . . ."

"What! You're sure?" Andy's mind reeled at the possibility of a mistaken identity, after all.

"Sure she was. Over the suit. This Clive, the guy in grey, he brought her a coat and a hat. Didn't I tell . . ..?"

"Ha!" Andy groaned. He took hold of Vince's jacket and nearly held him off the ground. "What else didn't you tell me?"

The proprietor of the store said in thin sceptical tones, as if to say he had come into the middle of the picture and didn't care for it, "Excuse me . . ."

"Wait a minute. Did you see such a girl?"

The man pursed his lips. "Couldn't say. Listen, I want to watch this show. If you'll excuse me . . ."

The light changed. Traffic moved.

Andy stood still. "Where did Clive *get* the coat and the hat?"

"He went into a house after them, the first time I . . ." Vince swallowed and shut his mouth suddenly.

Andy said, "I thought I'd seen you someplace before." He towered. His eyes bored down.

"Yeah, I just remembered myself . . ."

Andy's fingers met hard on Vince's arm. "You were parked around the corner. I even asked you . . . You had Laila Breen in your cab *there, then!*"

"Yeah, but she . . . she . . . she didn't want to be seen, she said, and listen, I thought . . . I didn't know what was up. I thought . . ."

Andy said bitterly, "I don't care right now what you

thought. No time for that."

"What'll you . . . ?"

Andy was hurrying across the street once more. He had made a complete square, now, and he pounded past the trailer. He went up the path. He bounded up the porch steps. He rang the doorbell.

Vince panted after. "Mr. Talbot, I feel terrible. I don't want to think it's any of my fault. Listen, what are you going to do?" His eyes wagged nervously in their sockets.

Andy said, bitterly, "Me? I'm going to use the telephone."

Clive stopped his whispering. Somebody was working the doorknob, yanking and heaving on the door. Clive's arm tightened and Dee thought her throat would break. They could hear men's voices.

"Hey, Al . . .?"

"Yeah?"

"You working in this service room. You lock this door?"

"Lock? Naw."

"I saw you close it."

"So OK. So the owner wants that door closed. Baxter does. Said so. He don't want the junk in there to show up in the picture."

"You musta pushed the button in the door or something . . ."

"Naw. Crash outside made me jump, gave it a bang. I remember. Get going, Coolie. Bowman's touchy tonight."

"I think he's nervous as a cat."

"What'd you mean, that door's locked?" The door rattled. "Heh, this is one of them locks, you can't get locked in. All you got to do is turn the knob in the inside."

"We can't turn the knob on the inside. Bowman's got a

bunch of keys, ha'n't he?"

"What's the difference, Coolie. Nothing was in there, I can tell you that."

Dee could not breathe at all. She was close to a faint. She might have moved her legs or her hands, but she was convinced that if she made so much as a rustle or a thud, she would faint and die. The madness in Clive was as mad as that. He was bound there would be no noise to betray their presence. He would not think about it. He would tighten the arm yet more, in a convulsive anger, and she could bear no more and she would die. She prayed for those men to leave, to go, to move away.

"So if it locks when I slam it," the man said, "nothing could *get* in, that's for sure. You going to let them put stuff on your face?"

"Not me, boy. Not me. I better see if Bowman's got this key. Say, what's the matter with my hat? If I want to wear my regular hat and keep that gook off my face, listen, I'm no actor! You stay on the back door, Al. Bowman's out front. . ."

"Stay outa *his* way, Coolie, or you're going to lose your hat, ha, ha. The boss don't want his customers to see that hat on TV. He's going to want you to look smart, boy. Ha, ha. You shoulda worn your tuxedo."

The men were moving, voices retreating. Then they were gone and Clive's arm relaxed. Dee gasped and choked and gasped again. And he began his whispering.

"I didn't hurt you, did I? I don't mean to hurt you, Dee. I wouldn't hurt anyone. I just want you to understand . . . You've got to promise me . . ." Clive writhed. "Got to," he sobbed.

He hated her. He wanted to hear Dee laugh. Dee say, "I believe you! I *know* you wouldn't do a thing like that! I'm sure of it. You couldn't!"

He had to hear it. "What, harm your little cousin, Laila? *You,* Clive? Never!"

He had to have it. Dee and her flaming faith could save him from all evil, and he hated her, because he had to have it.

Mr. Bowman said. "Well, *we're* all set. We're ready."

"Good." Mr. MacMahon of KROV was adjusting his earphones. "Won't be long, now. But you want to relax. Dave Ainsley will guide you, remember. Just talk naturally to Dave. He's done this a lot of times. He'll never let you down."

"It's sure an experience for me. But I'm mighty proud. Think I've got a very interesting story to tell the. . ."

"Sure. Sure you have. Excuse me. Testing."

Mr. Bowman took out his handkerchief and put it back into his pocket again. Stuff on his face, he couldn't mop it. He cast a nervous, baleful eye about, but then Dave Ainsley clapped his shoulder. "All set?" The young M.C. had a wide and friendly smile. "Your family looking in, Mr. Bowman?"

"Yes, my wife and her parents."

"Good. Good. And your customers, too, eh?"

"I hope so," said Mr. Bowman. "Ha, ha."

Dee, lying on the lumpy surfaces of the paper rolls, knew one outcry would be enough. The house walls were so thin that she could hear the men milling busily in the blaze of light outside. She could hear their voices, if not always the words, and one cry would have brought help to her.

But Clive's breath blew hot on her cheek, and lying

there, with an oily rag between her tongue and the roof of her mouth, trying not to strangle herself with the reflexes of revulsion, Dee listened to his whisper.

She was frightened. If she could have believed that Clive was strong for evil, cold of heart and head, she wouldn't have been quite so frightened. But he was not strong at all. His frantic weakness was her danger. It had been her danger while those men stood at the door. And it had been Laila's danger, all along.

He kept whispering, "Dee, I'm not going to do anything bad. I don't want to hurt anybody. But you've got to listen to me before you listen to Talbot. It was all mixed up, I tell you. Everything was just as you say — kind of catch-as-catch-can. It's not what Talbot thinks. At first I thought the poor kid was running away because of her feelings. I didn't see why I shouldn't help her. You understand that, don't you! If you do, just nod your head. Please, Dee. Nod your head."

Dee nodded her head and nodded it again.

"All right. It wasn't until that cab-driver . . . that's when I first *heard* about the poison. Don't you *see?* When I realised . . . listen, Dee, after that, didn't I do my best to find her? You know that, don't you? If you're not going to remember *that,* Dee, and be on my side. I don't know . . . I don't know . . . Now Talbot's got hold of that driver and you know what he was trying to insinuate. I'm not going to have it, Dee. Not going to have that kind of trouble."

He was half sobbing, half whining. *He's mad,* she thought.

"How would you feel if they started to say that you wanted your cousin to die? You and I are the heirs. You're the same as me. How would you feel?" Dee rolled her head. "You do believe me, don't you? Nod if you do."

She nodded.

177

"Nod if you'll be on my side. You'll make Talbot lay off. You won't . . ."

She kept nodding.

Clive's breath sobbed in. Dee was his only key to salvation, now. If the stubborn belief she'd shown in Talbot could shine for Clive, all would be well, somehow. And still he hated her because he had to have it and he couldn't get it. There was no way he could be sure.

"No, no," he said. "You've got to nod yes to everything just to get away from me. I know. You think everything is black or white. I can't trust you. Dee, listen, what I was doing, out there by the hedge . . . I was watching. Talbot and the cab-driver were on the trailer."

Talbot! Andy! Her heart jumped and Clive knew it. He wasn't sure why. His whining whisper was dying lower and lower in despair. He had enough clarity of mind left to know he couldn't ask her if she'd seen the gun because that would tell her that he'd had a gun. The rest was darkening.

"Dee, how can I trust you? Listen, Dee, if Laila gets sick or whatever it is . . ." he ducked his head and wiped his face on his sleeve, "it won't be my fault. Swear you believe that. Dee, I *want* to let you go!"

Dee knew he couldn't let her go. He was in a corner from which he could not escape. He was guilty. In every breath he gave it away. And nothing could save him from the guilt he knew, whatever the law might someday say. Clive was disintegrating, now, in his own horror at the mess he was in or the mess he was.

What he might do to Dee, herself, would bear no relation to logic or plan. He was as good as a madman and no one was going to come running to save her, either. Nobody. Not Andy Talbot. He probably thought she was in that hospital. Or, if he knew better, he still could not know where she was instead. Nor Dr. Stirling. How could he

178

imagine! Not the police. Nobody.

Oh no, Dee Allison would attend to everything in the flesh. Dee, the red-headed little fool, the busybody . . . She could have called the police — used the telephone still more — and then gone to bed in that hospital.

Well, no use wishing she had not run pell-mell into this jam. Because she had, and here she was. One thing was certain. She had better see what she could do to get herself out of it. So she set her will upon the problem.

No way to speak with Clive, reasonably or soothingly or even deceptively. He didn't dare let her speak, lest she scream. In that fear he was justified. She would scream as soon as ever she could. Meanwhile, he was dangerous. At any moment he could seize her throat again and press too hard. And time was passing. Dee couldn't find Laila until she got out of this, nor even try.

She stopped listening to Clive at all. In the strange light, she studied this tiny cluttered place. She began to feel about with her two feet, which Clive had tied together at the ankles. Her toes were sentient in the soft shoes. She used them like finger-tips. Sitting on the rolls of paper, leaning as he was over her, braced by an arm on either side of her body, Clive could not see what her feet were doing.

The light — wings, shafts, planes — penetrating by the cracks around the window and at the top of the window-frame, was very odd and confusing. But her shins came up and touched that step-ladder, that was leaning against the opposite wall. Carefully, her toes examined it. The legs of it lay between the rolls of paper on the floor. The rolls, however, were parallel in such a way as to leave each leg in a slot that pointed to the wall. Dee thought it out very carefully.

If only her weight and Clive's on the fat rolls did not count too much and wedge those rolls together, if the ladder could slide, if only the slots between the rolls were clear

179

to the wall, and the floor not too rough, and the angle at which the ladder rested sharp enough, and the room large enough, so that when she shoved with all her force at the ladder's bottom rung, it would slide to the wall, be vertical, then fall . . .

If Clive were surprised enough not to be able to duck away, the upper end of the ladder might hit him with some force. It might hit Dee, of course, but not if it hit him first.

It would, she decided, at least be noisy. It would be better than *this*, whatever happened. It was the only chance that she could see to do anything.

So she struggled as if she begged for speech and her eyes kept his face, as if she pleaded, and Clive kept sobbing.

"You stand up for me, Dee . . . or I . . . or I . . . please . . . I can't take any more—"

She thrust her toes on the ladder, knees bent, and she thrust both legs out with all her might. It worked better than she had imagined. The legs of the ladder were not wedged between the rolls of paper at all, but slid slickly in shallow grooves. The ladder reared higher, balanced forever. When it fell the sound was not much. The thud with which it fell was soft. The ladder was short enough. The room was wide enough.

It worked out nicely. Dee lay crushed under Clive and the ladder. But it had hit the back of his neck, she thought, and he was not whispering any more.

"Beaned him!" she thought exultantly. "Pretty good, Dee! Pretty smart! Atta girl!"

Now all she had to do was get that doorknob . . . or get someone's attention. So she began to squirm and struggle and strain.

Chapter Twenty

"What good I can do *here,* I don't know," said Talbot's despairing voice into Mrs. Gilman's phone. "There's absolutely no sign. If Laila was ever in that trailer, Pearl must have dumped her somewhere. I'm going to St. Bart's. See what I can get from Pearl. And see Dee."

"Dee's all right," the doctor said. "She called Lorraine. Now hear this, Talbot. Pearl told Dee that Laila was *in* the trailer."

"She did?"

"And Clive put her there. Do you get that? Where *is* Clive?"

"Gone," barked Andy. "This makes a big difference. Pearl says she was in it at the time of the crash?"

"So I understand."

"I'll call you," said Andy abruptly. He hung up the phone.

"Hey, Talbot—" Dr. Stirling shook his head.

Andy looked around the little house he was in. "Thanks for the phone," he said to this nurse or whatever she was. "You're positive you didn't see that girl?"

"Oh no. The police were asking me that very same thing," repeated Agnes Nilsson, in her most refined voice. "But, as I say, Mr. Talbot, I went immediately to the scene and did my best to give first aid. People are so often impulsive and although they mean to be kind, they will do the wrong things for an injured person. I felt that with my experience . . ." She spoke on. Andy had not long listened to her words.

The little sitting-room was old-fashioned and stuffy, windows curtained to the point of smother, furniture shabby and crowded, all dominated by the gleaming modern cabinet of the set. The nurse had turned the volume low, but the grey faces were jawing and fluttering busily, just the same.

The old lady's wheel-chair was drawn before the screen, but she was not peering at the world through that tiny window, just now. She was strained around, instead, to look backwards and her fingers were drumming on the chair's metal arm. Vince, who had shuffled slyly into the room and was watching the pictures, gave her a helpless grimace, with little attention in it. He dismissed her from the thinking world. The old lady's fingers seemed to flout and despise him.

Andy said forcefully, "Now, I *know* she was there, it's obvious to me, since Laila Breen had to get out of the trailer on the side toward this house, only someone near this house could have seen her. But if you rushed . . ."

"I ran down the steps. I happened to be on the porch when that coupé . . ."

"You couldn't see into the trailer at all?"

"No, I don't believe so. My attention, naturally, was fixed on the actual crash. It was all so sudden."

"Your patient," said Andy, "seems to be trying to attract your attention now."

"Oh well," said Agnes. "She wants to get into the act," she said in a malicious whisper. Her descent into a cant phrase was cynical and shocking. Andy's eyes flickered.

"Is she senile, Miss Nilsson?" he asked softly.

"The doctor says not," said Agnes brightly, but her eyes said, I've often thought so. You may have guessed it.

182

"A stroke?"

"Mrs. Gilman was injured in an auto accident some years ago," said the nurse primly.

"Injured in her mind?" pressed Andy.

"To a degree," said the nurse judiciously. "That is, she is very limited, of course."

"She can't speak?"

"No. No, she can't."

"She watches TV?"

"Oh yes," Agnes trilled. "Incessantly."

"Then her eyesight is not in question?"

"Why . . . uh . . ."

Andy said, "Where was she, during the accident?" He could see that the old lady's hand was listening, now.

"On the porch," said Agnes stiffly. "It was unfortunate. I've been a little concerned about the effect. However, she doesn't seem to have been too much affected. I've kept her quiet, of course. Perhaps she hasn't quite realised . . ." Her head nodded suggestively.

But Andy, looking at the old lady's hands, saw that it had left off its urgent tapping. It stretched out, stiff with her listening. It seemed to him that the fingers grew tense with imploring. Now, as he watched, the fingers closed, the hand turned over and dropped in despair. It was an eloquent hand. Surely it was attached to a mind.

Andy said, "Excuse me."

"I don't advise . . ." said Agnes, her voice rising.

"I must ask her," he said impatiently.

"I must insist . . ." Agnes moved into his path.

He looked at her. "It ought to be plain to a two-year-old that she wants to say something."

"Sure she does," said Vince suddenly.

"Did the police question her?" Andy was sharp.

Agnes said, "No, and while she is in my charge, I must

183

be the judge."

Andy said, "It's a free country, Miss Nilsson. This is her house, isn't it?"

"She must not be excited."

"G'wan, she *is* excited," said Vince Procter. He was getting in on this. His brown face was shrewd.

"All the more reason . . ."

The old lady's hand was saying, Alas! You see?

"Excuse me, Miss Nilsson," said Andy firmly. "If she wants to communicate with me, I'm afraid you are not going to stop it."

He walked around the wheel-chair and sat down and leaned close and looked into Mrs. Gilman's eyes, that were swimming with sudden tears. He said, "How do you tell me? Paper and pencil?"

She nodded. She dried her eyes on her fingers. Then her hand took the pencil. Vince came and leaned over the back of the chair. Andy craned his neck to watch the words grow black on the paper.

I saw the girl leave the trailer.

"Good!" Andy's voice vibrated with relief. "But did you see where she went, Mrs. Gilman?"

The pencil wrote, *Yes. Into a closed truck. A young man helped her into it. Closed doors. The truck went north. Paramount Linen Service licence number 72X3408.*

Andy said, "You are wonderful! I didn't dare to hope for such an intelligent and complete report." He touched her hand. "Now, I must telephone, right away. Then, I'll come and explain to you what it is all about."

Tears rolled down the old lady's cheeks.

"Now, she is very upset. You see!" hissed Agnes. "I'm afraid I must ask you to go, at once."

Andy said, hostilely, "Not until I telephone."

"She ain't upset," said Vince. He patted the old lady's

184

shoulder. He said, "Don't you worry," and he winked at her. He had taken a furious dislike to that big horsey nurse. He had a great need to be furious with somebody and he was grateful to this old dame for giving the information. He was glad that probably nothing bad was going to happen to the kid with the hair-do. So he sat down. He said to the old lady, "Say, what's this going on across the road? I bet *you* know."

Mrs. Gilman wiped her eyes. Beaming, she took up the pencil to tell him all about it.

Dr. Stirling read back the name and the number, the street and direction. "Not seven o'clock yet. Plenty of time. I'll have that truck picked up so fast . . ." Andy heard him sigh.

"Call me," he begged. "Take down this number."

"Got it." Stirling would have hung up but Andy said rapidly, "I'll tell Dee."

"Good. Get Clive."

"I'll get him."

"Hit him for me," said Dr. John and hung up fast. The compelling need to have Laila picked up was rushing him.

Andy hung up and held his head a brief moment. He ignored the fury in Agnes's eye. He dialled information for the number of St. Bart's. He thought, "Dee'll feel a lot better when she hears . . . She might even be happy." The thought of Dee, happy, made him wince somehow. Waiting, he thought, This Agnes and her big fat self-importance. Another *kind* of nurse here and they'd have found out, long ago — Dee was right. There's that difference — that's where, in all the complicated mess, we count. Each one. The *kind* he is. He began to smile ruefully to himself. What a time they'd be having with Dee, down there. She'd made them let her make a phone call. Perhaps by

185

now she'd be under sedation. It seemed strange to him to think of all Dee's bright force and energy quiet in a clean white bed.

Dee could not work the filthy gag away from her mouth. She could not cry out. Clive had bound her wrists together and her two hands were imprisoned under Clive's weight. She twisted and rolled and struggled to heave his weight away. If she could work out from under, get to her feet, or even to her knees, turn that doorknob . . . It was hopelessly high and far away. The ladder lay the width of the room. She began to fear it had got wedged, somehow, in her struggling, because she could not shift Clive's body which held her down.

Then Dee began to beat her heels on the paper rolls. But she could move her legs only from the knees, now, and her soft shoes made very little noise on the paper. Not enough noise. Not enough.

She used her eyes again, to search for a way to noise, for something else she could make fall and crash. Something that would bang. Her head, straining on the neck, bumped the sharp corner of a smallish box. She rolled her head and her eyes to look at it. The box was too near to be seen very clearly. But in a little while, she was pretty sure it was an old portable radio.

Her head slid. Her cheek felt the cold knobs on its face. She thought, Noise? If a radio began to play in here, surely someone would come to see why.

Chapter Twenty-one

Frank Turner had his ear stretched a mile, but she was still quiet. Sometimes he had a funny feeling that she might have disappeared; maybe she had been a dream he'd had; maybe he was the one who was asleep. Mike Torres still didn't have any idea that they had a passenger. Mike was giving a lecture, now, on safe driving, illustrated by an analysis of the crossroads crash behind them. Mike was a good guy, but preachy.

Frank let him go on but he wasn't listening. He was wondering what was *best* to do about the girl if she was real and hidden quietly behind them and no dream. He had well considered letting her sleep and ride secretly all the way to his house and he could still do it.

But Frank knew now this was a dream and could not come to pass. Mike had to be told about the passenger and Frank would probably get fired. And he thought he'd better tell Mike about her pretty soon. It was getting to be nearly seven o'clock already. Time to stop and take her on a bus. . . .

Still, they weren't anywhere near a bus, right now, that was going where she wanted to go. He didn't know yet if she wanted to go anywhere besides that hospital in Long Beach.

He could still take the girl home and telephone about that friend who got injured. *She* shouldn't go running around the city after dark. Let her, say, get a good night's rest and then, maybe, set about taking her where she be-

187

longed, if, on this earth, she belonged anywhere.

But Frank straightened his shoulders. He got stern with himself. The thing to do first was to find out what *she* wanted. Why she was so kinda scared and lost. What he ought to do to help *her*. So he had better let Mike know about it right away and take a beating, probably, but then he could ask her.

He thought she must still be asleep. He let a certain sweetness in the vision keep him silent for another mile.

But he got stern. You had to. You can't drift around dreaming in this world. It was best he found out. Wouldn't be very helpful to drag her too far out of *her* way, whatever it was.

So Frank said, "Say, Mike, I did something I got to tell you. There's a girl in back of this truck."

"Wha . . . !" The truck swerved to the kerb in righteous wrath. Mike Torres was about to blow his top and cite a million rules and regulations. Frank waited quietly.

But when he met Mike's eye, Mike certainly surprised him. He said quietly, "O.K., kid. You had a reason. What was it?"

"She was scared," Frank said, "and she asked me to help her."

Mike closed his eyes prayerfully. When he opened them the boy was still sitting there, still meaning every word of it. Mike let his mouth go lopsided. He didn't know! What could you *do?*

"You got plans?" he inquired.

"I want to ask her what I can do now, whatever she wants," said Frank serenely. "I was thinking I could take her home with me if she's got no other place to go."

Mike gave his cap a whack that sent it over his eyes. He slipped down the seat. "Pinch me," he said sourly, "but don't wake me. Listen, you're going to be out on your ear when you wake up. You know that?"

"I know," said Frank with a grateful grin on his face. Then he was stretching his body across the interim space and peering over the barrier. "Hi! Are you all right, Ma'am?" Mike heard him saying.

Mike hit himself on the top of the head and drove himself deeper into the seat. *He* didn't know . . . ! He was so late already, he couldn't bring himself to get excited. So the kid was crazy. It made a nice change, anyhow.

Mike's conventional gloom was rent. These kids! These damn kids! Good thing there were these kids in the world, maybe, after one generation grew up and got sour . . .

Frank was sliding over the wooden partition. She was lying against the linen bags and she was awake. There was just enough light to see that she smiled at him. He picked up her chilly little hand.

"We're quite a ways away, now," he said, "from the man who tells lies. I was wondering where you'd like to go."

"Aren't we going to the hospital?" He felt her hand tighten nervously.

"Well, we can. Sure. I found out which one. And Mike says the red-headed girl wasn't hurt very much. Is it the red-headed girl . . . ?"

"It's me," she said.

"Why, don't you feel well?" he asked in pure wonder.

"I do. I feel very well, but . . . but they are saying on the radio that I've been poisoned."

Frank felt his own startled frown. He believed her, though. Sure, he believed her. It was necessary to him to take every word she said as perfectly true. He had to, because she was an angel, and if he didn't believe her perfectly, why then she'd stop being an angel. "Did you hear that on the radio yourself, Ma'am?" he asked respectfully.

"Yes."

"Your name, and all?"

"Yes, and my clothes, my hair. It was me," said Laila,

earnestly.

"Well, then," said Frank after a stunned moment, "I'd better take you to a hospital."

Now her hand was warmer and holding to his tightly. "I was afraid at first," she confided. "I don't feel as if I'd been poisoned, you see, and I thought it might be that they would want to hurt me. But you don't think so, do you? You think I ought to go back, even if it is a mistake?"

"If there is any question," he said carefully, "sure. You should go and find out about it and make sure. It could be a mistake."

"I'm a little bit frightened. I don't understand it very well."

"I don't blame you for that," said Frank. He was feeling his path straight through the fantasy, the unearthly feeling. . . . "Is it any special hospital you want to go to, Ma'am?" he asked respectfully. And she told him. But he, suddenly alarmed, put his hand on her cheek, which was warm and delicate and soft . . . and as he did so, a roar came alongside and a loud voice said, "You got a girl named Laila Breen in this truck, Mac?"

"Huh? Whatsat, officer?"

The girl's cheek pressed Frank's hand. "Yes, that is my name."

Laila Breen. Frank remembered dimly having heard it before. He let her go and stood up and over the partition he said to the policeman, "She's here. She wants to go to the Greenleaf Hospital. Dr. Stirling."

The cop climbed off his motorcycle, put a foot on the truck, gave Frank a long hard stare, and then he stretched in and looked over. "Long black hair. Yeah. Well . . . she's going to the hospital. And so are you," he snapped at Mike Torres, as if he, too, felt that unearthliness and resented it and had to snap at somebody. "Follow me, Mac. I'm taking you through lights. Get rolling."

"What the hell am I? An ambulance?" yelled Mike over the wail of their escorting siren. "What's the *matter?* Why am I *doing* this? Somebody . . . hey, Frank . . ."

But Frank didn't answer. He had his arm around the girl in the blue coat, and he was saying he'd go right along with her, of course, so she needn't be scared and everything would be all right, he was pretty sure.

Andrew Talbot's palm sweated on the shank of the telephone.

"What do you mean, she ran away! You mean you let her go without treatment . . . without exam—" He listened a while longer and then hung up abruptly. "She didn't run *away,*" he said out loud. "She'd run right back into it."

Vince Procter had turned the sound higher on the TV set. He and the old lady had their heads together in a companionable sort of way. Fanfares and introductions, the sing-song swing of the announcer's spiel, were filling the little sitting-room.

Andy went marching to the front door, threw it open and looked out. Across the road, the show was ready to go ahead. The Baxter house, embraced and glorified by light, was the stage, and the dark figures of the onlookers stood in a thicket around the light's edge.

Agnes Nilsson followed him out to the porch. She said, angrily, "I must ask you to take your friend and go. I cannot permit any more of this excitement. I am responsible to Mrs. Gilman's sons and if you do not leave, right away, I'll have to call someone who will make you leave."

"Not yet," said Talbot briskly and coldly. "I'm expecting a phone call."

"Here?" She was outraged.

"Yes, here. So you'll have to put up with us a while." Her eyes glittered angrily, but Andy continued, "A girl I know may also be coming along . . ." He scanned the crossroads. The brilliance across the way made it difficult to see much else.

Agnes was swelling as if she would explode, so he said to her coldly, "If you will listen while I explain to Mrs. Gilman, I believe that, as a nurse, you'll see why all this is necessary."

He went back into the house. He touched Vince's shoulder. "Do something for me?"

"Yeah?"

"Go outside and keep a look out for Dee Allison."

"Huh?"

"She got away when that ambulance reached the hospital. She evidently wasn't hurt much. If I know her, she'll be trying her darndest to get back here into the thick of everything. You'll recognise her? Redhead."

"The one who was with you in the car?"

"The one with me."

"I'll know her," Vince said, saluting. "Sure. I'll spot her." He licked his lips with some relish. "Say, did you know that stuff on the TV screen is taking place right out there? Whadd'ya know, eh?"

Andy glanced at the screen. A man was standing beside a vehicle of some kind. He was being interviewed. He was very much pleased about it, stuffy and pompous, in his best clothes.

Andy turned Vince's chair, setting its back to the screen. He began to talk earnestly to the old lady. When Agnes Nilsson came in, she turned the TV sound down to an indistinguishable murmur, before she drew near to listen while Andy explained. About the toxin, the housekeeper's collapse, the disappearance of Laila Breen, the plight she was in, the hunt for her, the reason and the urgency.

The siren whooped into a hospital courtyard. The linen

truck looped after it. Mike sprang down to open the back doors, but Frank lifted her down.

A little later, Dr. Stirling found the young man in the waiting-room. "She'll do," said the doctor. "I think so. We got the antitoxin into her in good time." The doctor made a lip sound, a sucking in, the equivalent of a whistle. "I've got a feeling that there are some thanks due to you, young fellow. Maybe you don't know there was an old lady who ate that same contaminated salad. She died half an hour ago."

Frank looked very earnest and pale. "I didn't do anything. I'm glad that it's all right. I hope it is."

"It was in time."

"Luck, then," Frank said. "Just luck, sir. I was pretty stupid, as a matter of fact. Say, could I . . . ?"

But the doctor bent his brow inquisitively. "Now, you did something. She tells me that when she heard the broadcast, she was afraid to come. How were you able to teach her different, in so brief a time?"

"I don't know, sir," Frank said. "Of course, she was scared for a reason. I mean, it seems she happened to see some doctor use a hypo on her father when he died and she didn't understand, sir. Of course, I explained that, but it . . ."

The doctor goggled. "Of all the non—!" He snorted. "You . . . explained it? How?"

"I didn't exactly explain it," Frank said, swallowing. "I just told her, probably the doctor was trying to save him. I said doctors don't know everything but they always try the best they can. I mean, in *my* experience."

The doctor swallowed. And Frank went on: "I guess even before that she trusted in what I said. I'm glad if she did."

The doctor cleared his throat. He coughed.

"*She* didn't know," Frank said earnestly.

"All right, boy. I'll buy that. Doctors don't know everything." Stirling buzzed in his throat. It might have been

193

laughter. "Excuse me, I've got some phoning . . ."

"Could I see her?"

"You go right in," the doctor said with some warmth.

"Thank you, sir. There's one other thing."

"Yes?"

"I was thinking. If there's anything to pay," Frank said, "and she doesn't have any people or funds or anything, I'd be glad to take care of it."

The doctor stood still.

"If I could do it in instalments or something like that," said Frank, flushing. "I don't say I've got much on hand."

"What makes you offer to pay her bill?" the doctor demanded. "Isn't she a stranger to you?"

"Well, she asked me to help her and I said I would." The boy began to stammer. "I . . . I . . . I . ." His face was getting pinker. "I don't want to lose track of her, doctor. She well, since she did kinda trust me, I don't know how to explain . . . I've got a feeling she needs me."

"You might be right," the doctor said bluntly. He plunked his blunt hand on the boy's shoulder. "Don't ever forget that. Whatever you're told, whatever you hear, that's a little girl who needs somebody to . . . er . . . show her around. She's strange here."

The boy said, "She told me. She comes from an island. A little one, quite near New Caledonia, she said. She doesn't understand it, here. I thought she was an angel," he blurted. "I mean, I knew she must have come from some different place. She's . . . different, isn't she?"

The doctor said, gruffly, "You better go in. She and I don't want to lose track of you, either."

"Could I call my mother?"

"You can do anything you want to," bellowed the doctor, and went trotting down the corridor toward his office.

Chapter Twenty-two

"Talbot?" barked Dr. Stirling a moment later. "Laila's here. She's had the shot. She'll do, I think."

Andy Talbot groaned his exquisite relief.

"There's a boy here," the doctor said in an odd voice that was not brusque but flat with a kind of helpless amazement. "Well, never mind. . . Where's that Clive?"

"I don't know. Could Laila tell you anything?"

"That skunk," raved Stirling, "put her in the trailer and bolluxed Pearl's radio. There is no doubt at all that he knew what he was doing. Not only that, he saw Dee and Pearl into the ambulance and did not so much as mention Laila. Not only that, he saw Laila in that linen service truck and he let her get carried off in it. He is guilty as sin. He wanted her to get lost and die. He's worked against us from the beginning. I don't know what we can do to him legally, but what I'd like to do . . ."

"Don't worry," said Andy, "when I get my hands on that . . . crumb . . ."

"You don't know where he's got to, eh?"

"Told you, he's vanished. Haven't found a single soul who saw him go."

"Probably running for cover. Probably hiding. Realises he was stupid and made a mess of it."

"He may be hiding," said Andy, "but he won't hide long."

"See what you can do," said Stirling. "You're younger

195

than I am. And listen, you've been in touch? How's Dee?"

"I wish I could get in touch with Miss Dee Allison," said Andy, "but it seems she skipped out on that ambulance."

"Yes, I know."

"You know? She's called you?"

"No, not again. She called Lorraine. Said then she was going back to the corner of . . . oh . . . Lemon Grove."

"Yes, that's what I've been hoping. I thought surely she'd turn up back here."

"I thought she had. You said you'd tell her. She hasn't? That's a long time ago, Talbot."

"I know it is." Andy was suddenly tense again.

"Of course, Dee can take care of herself," said the doctor.

"If she's not sicker than she thinks she is."

"Dee's got enough sense to know that," scoffed the doctor. "She's not Laila, remember. Probably she had to give up and sit down somewhere. Don't worry. Dee's O.K."

"I suppose so," said Andy somewhat less anxiously. But he sat there a moment when he'd put the phone down. It didn't seem likely that Dee would sit down somewhere. No, Dee was not Laila. Laila not Dee.

He left the phone and went in to the invalid. His smile was grateful. "Mrs. Gilman, I know you'll be glad to hear that everything has come out all right. It's all over. Laila Breen has been found. She is at the hospital and she is going to be fine." The old lady beamed and nodded and Andy said, "It's plain to me that you saved her life."

The old lady was happy. Very thrilled, very happy, happy enough to cry. She was alive!

"How we are going to thank you, I do not know," said Andy. His eyes flickered to Agnes Nilsson. "If there is anything at all that I can ever do for you . . ."

Agnes came gushing. "Oh, I am so glad to hear the

good news. It *was* wonderful of Mrs. Gilman, wasn't it? So clever. Won't her sons be proud?"

"They sure will," said Andy grimly, and he nodded at the old lady and he thought she winked one of her streaming eyes.

"Going now," said Andy. "Sorry if I've disturbed you, but it was well worth it, believe me. Now, I've got to go to look for a certain human louse, a man who did his best to keep us from finding Laila Breen in time. He's caused a lot of the difficulty. Happens to be her cousin and one of her heirs, you see. He's gone into hiding someplace . . . but I'll get him."

He patted the invalid's shoulder.

"Want this up, so you can hear it?" he asked courteously. He moved to the TV set.

"So glad there's been a happy ending," gushed Agnes. And Andy winked at Mrs. Gilman.

". . . nothing living can survive," the voice of the M.C. was saying. "Now that the house is entirely sealed, as we have shown you, the next step is the actual releasing of the cyanide gas. This is KROV, Channel 12, bringing you, every Wednesday evening, your fascinating programme *It's A Living.* Tonight we are televising the complete story, how Mr. John Bowman of the Bowman Exterminating Company, makes his living. Now, Mr. Bowman, if you will show our viewers one of the most dramatic moments of your business. . . ."

Andy Talbot stood at the front door of the Gilman house. His eyes were thoughtful on Agnes's face. "I'll see that her sons are proud of her," he said warningly.

Agnes said, "Of course. Oh, so will I!"

"And if I were you, I'd listen a little quicker when she

wants to get into the act. That's a fine intelligent old lady."

"Of course, she is. And such a dear! I'm so glad we were able to help you."

Andy said, dryly, "Yes, thank you." And he went out.

Agnes closed the door. She noticed at once that Mrs. Gilman's fingers were twittering and tapping again.

Agnes's nostrils dilated. She was tired of eating crow. It was easy to pretend that she hadn't noticed. Mrs. Gilman heard her walk away and go into the kitchen.

The old lady stared at her screen, bending forward, with the old scream in her throat.

"You take all precautions of course?" Dave Ainsley was saying admiringly.

"Naturally," said Mr. Bowman. "Everything is sealed, even the chimney. Then we leave a guard on the house overnight. That's so that no person can accidentally get in."

"Don't want to gas even a burglar, eh?"

"Not even a burglar, ha, ha. Now, this is the container from which we release the gas."

"In that cylinder eh? Pretty deadly, is it?"

"Oh, absolutely. Even a plant will die," said Bowman.

"Is that so?"

"Oh yes, anything that breathes. For animal life, death is instantaneous. For a plant, it takes a little longer."

Mrs. Gilman rolled her chair, she reached the table, she took a paper and pencil, she began to write. She was a witness. She had seen a man in a grey suit, that worried one, the one who was, of course, the wicked cousin. The one who was in hiding, now. She had seen him. She knew where he had gone to hide.

She did not suppose he was still in the Baxter house. And yet, he might be. So she wrote. The words came black on the paper. But she was all alone in the sitting-room. There was no eye to read what she was writing, and on the screen Mr. Bowman continued, his eyes glazed with pride and glory, to explain in detail his murderous business.

Dee Allison could hear Mr. Bowman's loud, happy voice perfectly well, right through the thin walls.

". . . all kinds of pests," Mr. Bowman was saying importantly. "Of course here, as I saw, we have an infestation of fleas. Which is quite a problem. Now, when we can seal a house entirely and let the gas do a wholesale job, you might call it, why, I feel better satisfied with the job. Not many exterminators use this method any more, but, properly handled, it is perfectly safe. Especially in an area like this one, where we have air. After twenty-four hours, we must release the gas but it will leave the house and be dissipated harmlessly."

"And everything in the house that breathes will be dead?"

"That's right," Bowman beamed. "We give a guarantee."

"You do?"

"And we make good on it. When the Bowman Exterminating Company says the bugs are gone, they are gone. Ha, ha. There will not be a living thing in this house."

"Suppose a mouse has a nest in there?"

"He had better move his wife and family in the next five minutes, ha, ha."

"Ha, ha."

"Ha, ha."

Dee could hear the laughter. She punched at Clive's limp flesh with her knuckles and knees. He would not respond. He was still unconscious from that blow. He

199

would not wake up. Until he woke, he could not call out. He could not make a noise.

She could not call out. She could make no noise but a low mutter in the bottom of her throat or the soft thud of her heels, and the men on the other side of the wall were absorbed, and very conscious of themselves before the cameras and the microphone. They were not listening for soft thuds and mutters in this house, sounds no louder than a mouse might make.

"I, myself, release the gas of course," Mr. Bowman was saying grandly. "I never let anyone else do that. Now, if we can move around to the front door, which has not yet been sealed, why I . . ."

"I think we can get a look in through the front door. All right." Dave Ainsley's voice changed. "Ladies and gentlemen, this is your fascinating programme *It's A Living.* We are about to watch Mr. John Bowman of the Bowman Exterminating Company demonstrate one of the interesting and dramatic things he does to make a living."

Dee Allison worked in the striped dark to turn by the muscles of her eye-socket the knob on the old radio. For Clive would not wake. And nothing more would crash or fall. She worked by the friction of the skin of her cheek and the gag that was bound across it to turn the knob on the old radio. She thought to herself with desperate mirth, How will they figure it, when they find us? Will they say Clive murdered me? Or that I have murdered Clive?

She had no hope that anyone was looking for her, here. She had some hope. She remembered a voice had said it was going to ask for a key. Although that was long ago. A better hope, if she could turn this knob. If the radio had a battery with any life in it, then there would magically be some sound.

No one but herself to do anything about it. No Andy,

200

earing to heaven *she* would not die. Dee's bright hair
rred. She was not licked yet. The muscles of the eyes
at hold a monocle were not strong and would not turn
e little knob. But she began with courage to try once
ore to get her hands out, somehow, and turn the radio
.

Chapter Twenty-three

Talbot came up beside Vince, careful not to look at th[e] lighted house, since its brilliance would blind him to a[nything] else at the crossroads. He murmured the news, "Lai[la] Breen's been found. They've got her. She's O.K."

"Say," said Vince, "am I glad to hear that. You're gla[d] too, eh?"

"Yes. Haven't seen Miss Allison?"

"Nope."

"Or Breen?"

"Not a sign of him."

"Forgot to say, I guess I don't really need you," And[y] said. "There's no doubt, any more. Breen was in it, just a[s] we thought."

"That so? What a louse, eh? I'd still like to see him g[et] his, Mr. Talbot. I'm going to hang around, watch this pr[o]gramme. If I do see him . . ."

"You haven't been seeing anything *but* the programme[,]" Andy chided, "staring at that light." He turned his ow[n] back on it.

Back in the Gilman house, Agnes Nilsson marched pa[st] the wheel-chair with her mouth in a hard line. She turne[d] off the set in one angry snap. As the scene died off the tube['s] end, she said sternly, "Mrs. Gilman, I'm sorry, but anyon[e] can see you are much, much too exhilarated. I just can't l[et] this go on."

Mrs. Gilman leaned forward and her eyes were com[-] manding.

"I'm very sorry if you don't like it," said Agnes haughtil[y] but your own health is my concern and more important than a silly show. And whatever . . ."

Mrs. Gilman was not moving a muscle or an eyeball. Her piercing gaze was steady and even threatening. She held the piece of paper out in her hand. Mrs. Gilman was alive, from head to ankles, and it counted. It commanded. Agnes huffed breath out. "What is it? What is it now?" In spite of herself, Agnes stepped across the rug and took the paper.

Andy saw her figure against the light in the door and then darkly running down. Traffic flowed between them but he could distinguish Agnes lifting and waving the bit of white paper. He raised his arm to hail her, to show her where he was. He would have crossed to her but Vince had his sleeve.

"Hey," Vince was saying. "I just happened to think . . ."

"What? Wait a minute."

Agnes was crossing.

"You know," Vince said, "he coulda gone in *there* to hide. My God, if he did! Mr. Talbot, they're going to let cyanide gas in that house."

"What?"

"Lookit, the *house!* On the programme!"

But now Agnes was there and thrusting the bit of paper into Andy's hand. He tilted it to the light. Mrs. Gilman had written on it, *"Tell Mr. Talbot I saw the man in grey go into the Baxter house by the back door."* Concise and plain. But not complete. Andy frowned. He said aloud, "But when?"

"When what?" Vince craned to see.

Andy read the sentence from the paper.

"This house? Is *this* the Baxter house?"

"It is," said Agnes stiffly.

"So what did I tell ya! And listen, if he didn't get out again . . ."

"In all this light," said Andy frowning. "Someone besides Mrs. Gilman must have seen him." Agnes kept a malicious silence. "Did you?" he demanded.

"I? No."

"When could it have been?"

"When?" Agnes smiled. "She doesn't say when, does she? You were so insistent, Mr. Talbot, I supposed I ought to bring that right over . . ."

"They musta checked," said Vince. "They always do. Listen, that stuff they're letting loose in there kills every living thing. I heard them say so."

Agnes looked queer.

"When?" pounced Andy. "You must have some idea when?"

"It must have been before those lights went on at all," she faltered. "Because I had taken her inside."

And said, "Thank you," icily. He swung to look at the Baxter house.

"They're not going to gas any person," she said scornfully. "Mrs. Gilman may be smart but it is not likely even she will save two lives in the same evening. Excuse me?" She went away.

Talbot walked nearer to the house. The cameras were close on the front door now. The bystanders had been drawn to a tight knot behind them. One camera was almost directly in the doorway, and shooting through the door.

Vince said, "This guy's an exterminator, see. They already showed how they block the windows and they nailed up this here kitchen door. The whole house is tight like that, Mr. Talbot. What if he can't get out?"

"He must have realised what was going on, long ago," said Andy crisply. "He could hear. You don't imagine he'd stay hidden in there and let himself get gassed to death."

"Well, no," said Vince nervously. "Not likely. Probably

204

ie ain't in there no more." His eyes gleamed in his nut-
brown face. He was intrigued by the possibility.

Talbot drew into the light that still blazed on this side
door. He went all the way across the narrow grass.

The other side of the wall, Dee's sweating fingers slipped
on the knob, but it turned. It turned at last! She dropped
her face upon the strong-smelling paper. If the radio had a
battery, if the battery had any juice, if the dial was set to a
station . . . now, soon, there would be a saving sound. She,
herself, listening until her ears seemed pointed, began to
hear men's voices.

"Listen don't monkey with that seal, Mr. Talbot,"
thrilled Vince beside him. "Because they're going to let a
deadly gas loose on the whole inside . . ."

Andy said, "Even if Clive Breen did slip in here to hide,
he's probably slipped out, long ago."

"Yeh," Vince said. "Say, though . . . kind of a louse, this
Breen, ain't he? Wouldn't it be sumpin if he should get ex-
terminated! Holy . . . Hey, that's poetic — !"

"Poetic justice," said Andy Talbot. "I see what you
mean."

"Can you beat that!" Vince cried, entranced by the dramatic dream. "Aw, leave it lay, Mr. Talbot. We don't *know*,
do we? Maybe he's in there. Maybe he ain't. Listen, he's
the crumb who was going to let this Laila get lost. So?"

"So he was," said Andy.

"Then it's practically an act of God. It's perfect!" cried
Vince. "He knew about her, see, and he didn't do a thing to
save her, did he? All right. So it's fair enough. What's *he* got
a right to expect? He should be done unto the way he did!
That's fair enough."

"Pipe down," said Andy.

The sweating skin of Dee's face, slipping on the wood of

205

the box, grew colder. Her lashes trembled and fell.

Clive didn't stir.

She could hear their voices but in here where she lay there was no sound.

Mr. MacMahon said crossly, "What's with those birds around at the side, George? Go tell them to shut up, will you? We're on the air. Don't they know that?"

George said, "Sounds like a crackpot to me. Get the sound of it?" They could hear the lift of Vince's excitement, the ranting quality.

"Yeah, in that case, somebody better handle them," said MacMahon nervously, "so they can't get on mike. Or we'll be cut off, if they should start with any religious stuff . . ."

"One of them's a husky type." George was on the slight side, himself.

"We'll get them," the little workman, Coolie, promised. "Me and Al. Listen, Mr. Bowman would be fit to be tied was he to get cut off the air. This I know."

"Sounds like one of those soap-box types all right," MacMahon groaned. "Everything happens to us. You go, too, George."

Dee's eyes were shut. She lay still. No sound came from the old dusty box that had once held a radio. Long ago, somebody must have taken the insides out, for fun, to play with. No magic now. No song. No selling spiel. Just silence.

The two workmen loomed up behind Andy and Vince and seized their arms. They yanked and moved their victims away from this spot, out of the light, away from the crowd, apart from the people. Vince struggled and a bystander's head turned briefly, but no one was drawn from the TV show.

206

Andy surprised his captors by saying quietly, "Listen to me a minute, both of you. There was a man hiding in that house. Did you see him leave it?"

"No man in there," scoffed Coolie, the little one in the hat.

"Naw, we been working here all afternoon," Al was scornful, too. "That house is empty."

"O.K., wise guys," said Vince, recovering from surprise to anger. "O.K. You know everything, you guys. That's all right with me."

"Hold it," said Andy. "Listen, I have a witness who saw him go in."

"Musta been Bowman."

"No, it wasn't Bowman. It was a man named Breen."

"When was this?" said Al, indulgently, using his strong arms against Andy's quiet resistance.

"*After* the accident."

"What accident?"

"What accident!" raved Vince. "You wise guys!"

"Cars. Smash-up. You heard it." Andy turned his head. "You told me you had," he said to the smaller man.

"Sure. Sure we heard that. So what, Mister?"

Vince struggled and started to say something shrill, but Andy said, "Hold it. Keep still, will you, Procter? Now, tell me this. You men were working here. Was this side door sealed at the time of that crash?"

"No, it wasn't," Coolie said. "Mr. Bowman wanted to show that on TV."

"A man could get in." Andy was calm and logical. "Now, could he get out on the far side of the house?"

"No, he couldn't," Coolie said.

"Will they check?"

"Sure. Sure." Al wasn't worried.

"We checked already," said Coolie a trifle nervously.

"Nobody's in there," Al said, "or believe me, he'd a sung

207

out, long ago."

"Leave it alone, Mr. Talbot," Vince said. "So O.K. So nobody listens. So this is going to be quite a programme, maybe. They start killing everything in there, they might find out . . ."

"Quiet," said the young man named George, coming up.

"Yeh, shuddup," said Coolie in sudden anger. "You! What's it your business?" He gave Vince a tug and then he said to big Al, "The onney thing is, Al . . ."

"You *did* check," said Andy.

Coolie ignored him. "Al, if you didn't monkey with the lock . . ."

"Naw," said Al, "I slam the door and it locks, that's all."

Andy was listening carefully. He heard doubt in the little man. His mind went to work on it.

"Innafearing with my freedom," yelped Vince. "Who you pushing around?"

"You've got no right to break up our show, you know," said George, "but you kinda people never think of it that way."

"Take it easy," said Talbot sharply. "For God's sake, nobody lose his head right now. And skip arguing your own business. Get this straight, can't we? What's this about a door locking?"

"What *is* this anyhow?" said George, puffing.

"We believe there may be a man in there."

"What's that!"

"Let him get gassed," croaked Vince. "He's worth no trouble."

George said, "Look, you two fellows checked, didn't you?"

"We did," said Al. "Nobody's in there."

But Coolie said, "I don't know. . . . ."

"Look," said George, turning pale, "if *you don't know,* I've

208

got to go say something."

"Lemme," said Coolie. "You hang on to this one."

"No, no. I'll go."

"You're nuts, Coolie," Al said.

"Tell them what we say," called Talbot after George.

"Yah. Yah, I'll tell them." George went scooting toward the front door of the house and drove into the crowd.

"Now, what's this," demanded Andy, "about a door?"

"Aw," said Al. "It don't mean a thing. There wasn't anything or anybody in that place when I slammed the door. So how could they get in later? See?"

"Yeh, but . . ." Coolie began and added weakly, "Well, anyhow, he'll tell them."

"You're satisfied, now, ain't you? That whatever's his name, George, he'll tell them?"

"It's no way to die," said Andy.

"Be all right for our crumby friend," leered Vince.

And Andy said sharply, "Cut it out, Procter. It's no way for any human being to die and you know it."

"Aw, Mr. Talbot, I don't really think he's in there."

"He ain't in there," said Al, "and you guys don't want to make a disturbance."

"Not at all," said Andy. "We'd just like to make sure you are not going to kill a man." He turned his head to look sharply at the smaller of these men.

Coolie, shifting from foot to foot, said, "The onney thing is, I . . . I . . . I . . . never did ask the old man for them keys. I didn't wanna . . . didn't wanna . . . didn't wanna take my hat off."

"Relax," said Al.

"What keys!" said Andy. "What about your hat?"

It took him a few minutes to understand. Slowly, he got the sense of the minor feud between Coolie and his boss. The triviality. Bowman wanted Coolie televised without the disreputable hat. But Coolie, in an inverted vanity, did not want to look other than his daily self. So, he had "forgotten" to ask Bowman for the keys.

"You mean you did *not* really check behind that door. You took a chance?"

"Naw," Al said. "There wasn't no chance. Listen—"

Meanwhile, the assistant, MacMahon, said into his communicating device, "Mr. Osborne, at least I've to get this to Bowman. Why don't I get him to fake the release of the gas? Then there's no harm done, and we don't hold up the show, either. How about taking the pictures off three, for five seconds? Dave can stall . . ."

"You're going to bust the rhythm of this thing," said the director, who was inside the control truck. "Who are those people? Nuts?"

"George says it was one of Bowman's own men who didn't seem positive. You better let me have five seconds with Bowman. Otherwise, I don't want the responsibility."

"O.K. Signal Dave. We'll take three, in five seconds."

Andy, held in the big man's hands as harshly as ever, said again. "Somebody better make sure they look behind that door."

The little man, Coolie, who was jittering up and down on the ground, suddenly let go of Vince and went plunging after George. As the assistant, MacMahon, slid through the front door of the house, Coolie caught George's coattails, "Listen, is he going to get the keys?"

"What keys? No, no. Going to get Bowman to fake the whole thing. So it's O.K. Don't worry."

"I don't *know,"* said Coolie. "Mr. Bowman, he don't know which end up he is, hardly. He's got his mind on all his friends and customers looking at him. I don't know if he'll get the idea even. You don't know Bowman like I do. Lemme get through in there and get the keys?"

"What keys?" asked George, and Coolie began to explain all over again.

Chapter Twenty-four

Camera number one, shooting through the wide open front door, caught the interior of the Baxter house, and two men in the middle of the front room floor with a wicked-looking cylinder resting between them. Then Dave Ainsley's eyes flickered. The screens in the living-room began to see through camera number three, a wide-angled view of the exterior, the house corner, and a slanting glance at the bystanders. "Ladies and Gentlemen . . ." smoothly Dave Ainsley began to recapitulate. MacMahon walked up to Mr. Bowman who was jolted and unsettled by the interruption. "We hear a man got in here," MacMahon said to him rapidly but firmly. "It's not sure he got out. Best if you fake that release, Mr. Bowman. Just pretend to open that valve. You can do that? Nobody will know the difference."

"There's no man in here," said Bowman, glassy-eyed and indignant.

"Can't take the chance, sir. Promise me you'll fake it. If you do that, we can continue."

"Yes, yes."

"O.K.?"

"Yes, O.K." Bowman stood, breathing a little hard. His eyes rolled down the vistas of the wide-open little house. He licked his lips and the taste of the make-up was on them.

"Camera will be back on you in a second. You understand, now?"

"Yes, certainly. Certainly."

As MacMahon withdrew, Dave Ainsley began: "And now Mr. Bowman is just about ready to show us how he does it. Mr. Bowman, you tell me this is fast, is it?"

Bowman began to speak with growing excitement. He was rapt and proud of his work and he was on the air the first and last time in his life. His hands gestured over the cylinder. "I wear a mask for this," he explained, "but I don't hang around, even so. I get out of here as fast as my legs can carry me. Anything that breathes, you see, is gone instantaneously. That's the beauty of it."

MacMahon glanced through through the open bedroom at the open closets. He slipped back through the little house. He touched the doorknob of the one closed door. He turned it, used pressure. Then he made a quick tattoo with his knuckles on the wood. He said, "Anybody in there, *speak now.*" But his ear on the wood heard no answer and no sound.

From the edge road where he was standing with Al's hard hands still on his forearms, Talbot could see the earphoned heads of the camera men rising above the crowded backs, and the solid crowd around the control truck itself peering in at the gadgets and the engineers, the matter-of-fact of the magical process. He could hear, at the crossroads, the drag of sudden interest and attention, a kind of hesitation step in the rhythm of traffic, as motorists noticed that something was going on here.

Al was saying, "So what? I'm telling you this guy was *in* the auto accident. That's what you say yourself. So how in hell could he be inside that room in there and me slamming the door when I hear the cars crashing?"

"You're certain the door was fixed to lock, *then?*" Andy was using his head, searching for a flaw in this reasoning. "Or did *he* fix it to lock, when he went in there to hide, *later?*" This big Al wasn't quick. "Was that door unlocked when you started to work in there?" Andy pounded, hunting for a fact. "Did *you* open it without a key?"

"Well, sure, because we hadda seal up in there. We hadda get *in.*"

"But it's locked *now.* Somebody messed around with it. Who? *You* didn't."

"Well, I — don't think I did. But I mighta — "

"For gosh sakes," Vince said, "the guy's got ears, hasn't he? And he ain't locked *in,* they say. He can walk out any time by turning the knob. You trying to say he's committing suicide, Mr. Talbot?"

"I'm remembering that he *was* in that auto accident and in one of the cars that crashed. It's possible he was hurt more than anyone knew. Suppose he passed out in there?"

Andy was thinking. Between this big dumb easy-going illogical type, Al, and that nervous feuding little one — worried about his pride — it could go wrong. Through the intricacy, he could see the zigzag possibility that led to death.

"Aw," scoffed Al. "That's hardly likely. Anyhow, I'm pretty sure the door locked when I shut it."

"Pretty sure," said Andy.

Vince, who was standing free, said, "Well, it's not our responsibility, anyhow. We done all we can do about it. I sure wouldn't want to go in there now, believe me. This programme must be pretty near over."

Now George came puffing back to where they were standing. "It's O.K.," said he gaily. "It's simple. The guy's

213

going to fake it. He's not going to let any gas out, that's all. See how easy?"

"Who ain't going to let any gas out? *Bowman!*" Al stiffened.

"Sure. So there's nothing to worry about. See? We don't want to throw the programme if we can help it. Naturally."

"What kind of a man is this Bowman?" said Talbot, sharply.

"He's O.K.," said Al. "He's O.K. I guess."

"Guess," said Andy.

On the screen, in the picture, Bowman said, "Now, Dave, I guess you better leave me. And you, too, Mr. MacMahon." He nodded off-stage. "I'll just attend to this little unveiling and we can leave the bugs to die. Ha ha." His hands fiddled with a gas mask.

"Mr. Bowman," said Dave Ainsley in his eager pleasing voice, "I want our viewers to especially understand the precautions that you take. Now the entire house has been completely inspected."

"Certainly," said Bowman.

"It's impossible for a pet or anything like that to be in another room for instance?"

Bowman bridled. "My men . . ." he began.

"Two minutes. Quit stalling," barked the director, in the control truck. MacMahon began to make time signals. He, himself, slipped toward the door. Mr. Bowman stopped explaining the careful routine of his faithful workmen and took a breath and put on his gas mask. Dave Ainsley began to walk backwards toward the door, where Coolie crouched under the camera, staring in.

"Relax, will ya?" Al rumbled. "They'll watch it. Anyhow, probably the man got out long ago."

"Probably," said Andy.

214

"Why sure. Been a long time since them lights went on. He's probably long gone."

"Probably'" said Andy again.

"Like I say, Mr. Talbot," said Vince the cab-driver, "it's no responsibility of ours. We told them. It's up to somebody else, now, I should think."

It was a soothing match. George soothed, too. "Smart thing to do is just what they're doing. Fake it. MacMahon thought of it. You get sharp in this business. You got to think fast. Nobody wants to get redheaded around a TV show, believe me."

"Redheaded?" said Andy Talbot.

"Just an expression."

"Expression. I see."

MacMahon, watching Bowman who stood ready in his mask, felt himself being tugged at. Coolie whispered, "Did you get the keys? Gimme two seconds, I can unlock that door."

"It doesn't matter. He's not going to let the stuff loose at all. He's going to fake it."

"Yeah?" said Coolie weakly.

"He was warned," said MacMahon. "I told him. It's his responsibility, now."

Coolie got up as if he were tired. He made his way out of the crowd.

"O.K.?" asked Al.

Coolie said nothing.

"Will he fake it?" asked Andy suddenly.

"I don't know," said Coolie. "Too late. Too late, now. He . . . he . . . he . . . gets concentrated."

"Well, too late now," said Vince.

Andy stared at the ground. He could hear himself saying reasonably, "I did all I could. I warned them. It was their responsibility, after that. I am not to blame." He hung there, loosely, in Al's strong and unrelenting hands.

He heard himself saying this to Laila Breen. Her brown eyes would hold a perfect trust. She would say, "Of course not Andrew," in her soft sweet voice.

But the redhead? A shocked tingling began in his blood. It wasn't good enough for Dee Allison. It was just not good enough. It would not do. You never stopped. You did not say, "I'm through."

He could feel big Al's paws tightening against his sudden tension and the big body bracing to hold him.

On the TV screens, and on Mrs. Gilman's among them, there was only one figure now, the man in the mask, and he was speechless. Off screen, Dave Ainsley's voice continued, working up the pitch. Making it exciting. Actually, there was nothing exciting to see. The man in the screen merely squatted down and his hands went to the mechanisms at the upper end of the cylinder, but Dave Ainsley got breathless . . .

Outside, on the edge of the the road, Talbot said quietly, "Say, Procter?"

"Yeah, Mr. Talbot?" Vince pricked up his ears.

"Remember what it was you said you'd like to see? When we caught up to Breen?" Andy was letting himself sag.

"Huh? Yeah, I . . ."

"We'd walk up to Breen, you said, the two of us. You'd give me a nod. Remember what I'd do, then?" Andy's voice was a drone.

"Yeah. Yeah, sure. I remember." Vince licked his lips. His eyes were squirrel-bright.

"Why don't *you* do it," said Andy, "to the man behind me, *now*."

So Vince, grinning as wide as his whole face, delighted with himself for catching on and with the drama of it all, didn't even stop to wonder why, he simply wound up a haymaker and cracked Al on the jaw with it.

Al only staggered but Andy got away. He brushed George from his path. "Sorry, gentlemen," he said calmly, "But I will have to go personally."

He slammed through the ranks of the onlookers.

Whipping before camera number one, he knocked it crooked; he knocked Dave Ainsley aside. The figure of Bowman stood up and gesticulated furiously. But, on the TV screen, there was a whoosh of jumbled light and shade and the picture vanished. Channel letters came on and stood stolidly.

Andy ran without breathing into the pantry, through it, into the kitchen, turned back, saw the one door that was closed in this house. Bowman was crouching over the cylinder. Coolie came flying in. "The keys!" he yelled. "Boss, boss, gimme the Baxter keys." Then Bowman ripped the mask off and began to roar and MacMahon had flung himself angrily on Talbot's shoulders.

But Coolie had a key in the lock and Andy yanked the door open. Breath rushed into him and he yelled in shock and fright.

Chapter Twenty-five

"Due to unforeseen difficulties . . ." a voice was droning. Mrs. Gilman sighed.

Agnes turned from the front door. "They're bringing some people out!" she cried. "Two unconscious people!"

"Oh, no!" said Agnes Nilsson under her breath. "Not three lives!" She looked into the sitting-room behind her, superstitiously.

Suddenly, the picture bloomed again on the screen.

"Ladies and gentlemen," Dave Ainsley was almost screaming with joy, "a most dramatic incident . . . Just as you saw Mr. Bowman about to release the deadly gas . . ." The picture wobbled on a mass of milling people and then it steadied on a girl, whose head rolled sleepily. Then it turned to a man, lying on the ground, who moved and tried to sit up.

The nurse and the invalid watched until Dave's last gasp, last wildly excited syllable died away and the music came on. Then Agnes asked timidly, "Is there anything else you would like now, Mrs. Gilman?"

Mrs. Gilman rested her head back. She was smiling faintly. She picked up her pencil and wrote, "No, thank you, Agnes. That's enough for tonight."

Some of the light remained, enough to shine on Dee's red-gold hair and her dirty animated face. She sat on the step of the Baxter house, leaning on Andy Talbot's shoulder.

"I sure outsmarted myself," she said. Her tongue was thick. "First I ran myself right into a jam, and then I had to go and bean him. Golly, was I glad to hear your voice!"

Andy said, appalled, "You could hear!"

"I think I passed out," she said. "I knew I was all right, then."

Nobody spoke. She looked where Clive, lolling on the seat of a police car, didn't seem to care that he had been got out or what they would do with him now. He looked beaten and empty and it was true, Dee thought, he could never be got out of the jam he was in. The silence grew on her. She looked about her. "A near thing, I guess," she said tentatively.

"I would have faked the release of the gas, of course," said Mr. Bowman haughtily. "I must say I don't like any of this." Mr. Bowman was going to sue somebody.

"I was about to cut the picture off the air," said MacMahon quickly. "We'd have to make sure . . . We never . . ." He choked.

Coolie said, "I was tryin' to get the key. All the time. I woulda yelled or something and broke it up. . . ."

But the night air tingled with alarm, just the same. With what might have been. Intentions, crystallizing *now,* coming into full existence as memories, were not yet as thick and firm and real-seeming as they would be. The tingle of fright still ran on the nerves, the tremble of self-doubt, memories of chances taken before, of conclusions jumped to, and bucks passed.

Dee drew a shaky breath. "Any more questions?"

The policeman shook his head.

She said, "We want to go to Laila, now, don't we?"

"Yes, we'll go. Here's Procter with his cab."

Andy helped her up gently. She was distressed. She could feel his distress.

Vince Procter couldn't get over it. He was enchanted that he had missed getting a bullet in his back by so narrow a margin. He himself had gone to find the gun in the bush. It was loaded. Now, he drove them with unconscious skill and over his shoulder the excited rehashing came like a scarf in the wind.

"Listen, who can tell, hey? Maybe he'd a taken a crack at you, too, Mr. Talbot. Guys like that go berserk. He mighta shot two — three people."

Vince was deliriously happy.

"Say, Miss Allison, how come you didn't yell? You coulda got shot, would you have yelled. You know that? How come you spoke like you did to him?"

"I don't know," said Dee and began to cry.

Andy said, "Look, she's been in a crash and pretty near choked and pretty near gassed — Let her have peace."

"O.K. O.K." said Vince, "but she's *my* girl! She's for me, this redhead! What I mean —"

"Be quiet," snapped Andy.

St. Bart's at Long Beach was discreetly crowded with quiet visitors. Pearl Dean plucked at the coverlet. "Laila is well," she said moodily.

"Yes, I know Pearl. I know you are glad."

"I am glad. So kind of you to come, Estelle."

"Dearest Pearl . . ."

"And your flowers . . ." The eyes rolled listlessly.

"They will breathe health, Pearl. Shall I call the nurse?"

"Do," said Pearl, brightening. "Miss Marlowe is a remarkable woman. To be a nurse, Estelle, is a noble proession."

"Do you think so, Pearl?"

"Selfless," said Pearl, "and wise! Ah, Miss Marlowe . . ."

"Hi, Miss Dean. How's my patient? What lovely flowers."

Estelle watched the clean hands jam the stems into the bottle and she winced, birdlike.

"There, now," said the nurse, bending over with her clean crackle. "Everything O.K.?"

Pearl said earnestly, "I know I am in good hands."

"She's a one," said Miss Marlowe with a cheerful smile. "An experience. I would not have missed . . ."

"Dear Pearl, to rise over your pain!"

"Go on, she's having fun," said Miss Marlowe, almost affectionately.

"You have never been ill a day in your life, Estelle," said Pearl, "or you would understand. The *caring* of your fellow creatures is such medicine to your soul . . ."

"She's a one," said Miss Marlowe, but her eyes were shining with both amusement and pleasure. This Pearl was a whack, to be sure, but the way she put things did make you feel kinda important.

In Dr. Stirling's smaller place, the Greenleaf Hospital, Laila sat upon a bed with her legs crossed tailor-fashion. Her hair was braided into two great long braids and a nurse had tied blue ribbons on them. Laila looked like a cute schoolgirl, and not the least bit exotic, and she was jabbering in a happy spate. But Frank Turner, sitting beside the high bed and listening gravely, had no doubt she was the same angel as before.

Her cousin Dee sat in the corner, all her splendid colour faded in weariness and bewilderment. She did not look at Andy, or the doctor, or even this boy, but at Laila's sparkling face, and the look in her eyes that was so curiously *not* reverent any more.

She knew Andy leaned over the bed, and heard him say, gently, "We must go, Laila."

She felt his touch upon her arm. "It's late, Dee."

"Yes." She pulled herself up. "I'll say good night, sweetie. Good night, Frank."

"Good night, Miss Allison."

Laila said, "Oh, good night, Andrew and Dee. But Frank can stay a little longer?"

"Sure he can," buzzed Dr. Stirling. "He's got privileges around here."

"I'm glad," said Laila demurely and her brown eyes slipped sideways in a look, as old as Eve, that no one had ever taught her at all.

"That's quite a lad, that Frank," said Stirling in the corridor.

"For which I thank the Paramount Linen Service, the United States Army, and God in his mercy . . ." said Andy with sudden vehemence.

"You're fired, Dee," chuckled the doctor. "Frank's going to raise her, whatever we do, whoever I hire. You're staggering. Go on home or I'll put you to bed here."

"And Clive?" she asked. "What shall we do?"

"Prosecute," said Stirling. "He's best where he is, in jail. I wouldn't let him loose on society."

"Poor Mrs. Vaughn," said Dee. "Poor thing."

"Take her home, Talbot."

So Andy put her in the car and Sidney drove them home. Lorraine, strong and kind, welcomed her mistress with affectionate gladness and went running up the stairs to draw Dee's bath.

222

"Go to bed," said Andy tensely. "You're not fit to be out of it."

"I know." But Dee sat down on the stairs in the same spot where she had been sitting so long ago. Her head bent against the spindles. She could smell the varnish. "Quite a day at the beach," she said without spirit.

"Dee."

"Yes."

"We found her."

"You found her, Andy."

"Who's to say who found her? We both did. Lots of people did, in a higgledy-piggledy way . . . "

"All right. But you were sensible."

"Dee, you tried to tell me how complicated it gets, all these intersecting lives . . ."

"I remember."

"I see what you mean."

"Do you?"

"There's such a thing as silly pride," he said.

"Yes."

"It's bad enough, it's hard enough, without *that*."

She didn't answer.

"Don't you think so?"

"It's hard enough," she said.

"Now, I could go away . . ."

She didn't answer.

"Too proud to trust you to understand. But Dee, you'll believe me."

"A long time ago," she murmured, "I think I should have just . . . believed you."

His voice gained power. "Then believe this. Ah, Dee, you're *my* girl. You're the one for me. If you can be."

"I won't be silly and proud *again*," she said.

He sat down and took her limp hand. "Things said,

mistakes I made, they hurt me enough," he said drearily, "I could run away."

But her voice had more life in it. "It's bad enough without that."

"You look beautiful," he told her gravely, "dirty and haggard and old. Nothing can blind me. I know you, now."

She moved her fingers.

"There's teaching, and then again, there's learning something," he said humbly. "There's the urge to take care . . . and a need to be taken care of. Ah, Dee, do both for me?"

She tightened her hand. She turned her bright head from the hard varnished wood to his breast.